SLADE

STELLA ANDREWS

Copyrighted Material
Copyright © Stella Andrews 2021
Stella Andrews has asserted her rights under the Copyright, Designs and Patents Act 1988 to be identified as the Author of this work.
This book is a work of fiction and except in the case of historical fact, any resemblance to actual persons, living or dead, is purely coincidental.

All rights reserved. No part of this book may be reproduced or transmitted in any form without written permission of the author, except by a reviewer who may quote brief passages for review purposes only.

18+ This book is for Adults only. If you are easily shocked and not a fan of sexual content then move away now.

18+

NEWSLETTER

Sign up to my newsletter and download a free book

stellaandrews.com

SLADE

Stella Andrews

Not every girl loves a bad boy

Slade

I have no heart.

I have no emotion.

I'm cold, broken and dangerous.

I like to hurt, cause pain, followed by the ultimate pleasure, then I walk away leaving broken hearts behind me.

Now I have a challenge, a beautiful, desirable, feisty woman needs my help.

She has asked for something most men would kill for but I'm not most men and when I'm finished with her, she will break like the rest of them.

Skye

I never wanted a bad boy. The only man I ever wanted was respectable, kind and safe.

Be careful what you wish for because dreams are often nightmares wrapped in rainbows.

I need help and I know just who to ask.

Slade Channing, the man I even warn myself about.

I almost think he'll refuse but will the payment he demands be something that destroys my future?

Yes, be careful what you wish for because once you make a deal with the devil, he sets fire to your soul.

PROLOGUE

SLADE

It feels strange being the only one in the Dragon's Ruin. The last Channing and the last member of my family running this bunch of surly bikers.

It's going take some doing, turning them into a club that's respected around these parts, but if it takes my entire life, I'm going to try at least.

"Hey, Slade, you fancy heading out to get something to eat?"

Marina pokes her head around the door and I shake my head. "I'm good thanks."

She looks concerned. "Are you ok, honey, you've been holed up in this office for days. I can't remember the last time you even came to the bar; the guys are talking."

"Fuck the guys, if they've got a problem, they can come and find me."

She doesn't take the hint and heads inside, perching on the edge of the desk, revealing she's not wearing any underwear. "Hey, we could…"

"Not interested, Marina."

The hurt in her eyes doesn't concern me because I have touched this woman for the last time.

"You always were a bastard."

"And you're only just finding that out."

"Come on, Slade, you pretend you don't care but there must be some part of you that wants a woman to love, someone to curl up with up at night and face the world together as a team. Someone like Sawyer and Billy found; it's not natural to be alone."

"I like it this way. Anyway, what's it to you? We hooked up a few times, big deal. Maybe you should concentrate on sorting your own shit out."

"I was trying to." She sounds so sad it should make me feel compassionate, to try to make her feel better, but it doesn't. I don't feel anything for this woman, in fact I've never felt anything for any woman and that's just how I like it.

She sighs again, which tells me I need to get the fuck out of here before I say something I'll regret because despite what everyone thinks, I do respect her position in this club. When Sawyer left and Axel took off, it was Marina who helped put the club together. She hired staff and cleaned up the joint. She organized the housekeeping and made sure everyone played by the rules. She has become a valuable asset, and I'd be a fool to upset her, but I won't give her me. I know that's what she wants, she tells me often enough, but I don't want a woman tying me down. I want my freedom.

"I'm heading out—alone."

Grabbing my jacket, I storm out and glare at a couple of Dragons who are smoking outside. "Make sure you call me if there's anything I need to know; I'm heading out on business."

Griffin nods. "Do you need company?"

"No."

I grab my helmet and ram it down hard on my head. Some prefer not to wear them; I love the anonymity it gives me.

As I ride, I feel the tension leave me as my speed picks up. It's the release I crave more than sex sometimes because out here, in the open, I owe nothing to nobody.

I must ride for a couple of hours before I end up at a place that I have yet to grab the courage to enter.

The Coyote Bar.

Since meeting my father's wife—Rose, I struggled to deal with it. That they never trusted me enough to tell me they were married, will never rest easy with me. The fact they told Sawyer; confided in him, hurts like crazy, but Rose is my last connection with Billy around here and it would be good to talk about him with someone; find out how he lived his last days from the person who loved him the most.

I hid it well, but I was blown away by the woman who stared me in the eye and told me something my own family were too scared to. I liked her. The trouble is, words don't come easy to me and I'm not one to put my feelings out in the open. So, I've been brooding on that the past three months while I've tried to clean up the Dragons, but I'm finding it harder to stay away.

The sound of a motorbike grabs my attention and my heart sinks when I see Devon, the President of the Dark Lords rolling into the car park. I doubt he's seen me from my place in the shadows and I watch him, wondering why he's here.

He takes a while before he gets off his bike and lighting a smoke, leans against the wall as if waiting for someone. He doesn't appear in a hurry and many customers pass him looking worried because he is not the sort of customer this place needs.

I decide to stick around to see what happens because it's obvious he's here for something—or someone.

It must be fifteen minutes later that the bar door opens and I see Sky, Rose's niece, look at him furiously.

He pushes off the wall and heads her way and if anything, she looks angry and I laugh to myself. I met her once, but that was enough to make one hell of an impression because that girl is the finest one I've seen around these parts. Long blonde hair pulled high in a ponytail and the bluest eyes I have ever seen. Her waist is small and her tits are huge and her curves are the blueprint for perfection everywhere. Long tanned legs end at an ass I could easily ruin, and I'm not surprised Devon is looking at her like she's the goddess of sex.

She waves her hand and is obviously angry with him, and yet he appears to find it amusing.

After a while, he holds up his hands and walks away, and she slams the door behind her as she heads inside.

To my surprise, he passes by his bike and heads my way, and I'm guessing the bastard knew I was here all the time.

"Slade."

He nods and hands me a cigarette and laughs. "That will keep me going until the next time."

"From here she looked mighty pissed. What's the story?"

"There isn't one—yet."

"What do you mean, yet?"

Devon grins, but it's an evil one as he puffs a plume of smoke into the night air. "I've got my sights set on that wild cat and I'm not about to take no for an answer."

"Even if she's not interested?"

"She will be."

He looks at me with a hard edge to his stare. "What's your business here?"

"Not sure, just seemed like a good place to get some air."

Devon throws me a look that tells me he's not buying a word of it. "You know, Slade, we've always got on ok, so I know you're not gonna care what I say next."

"Depends what it is."

"It's good you took over the club; we'll work well together. I know you need to build members up and if I hear of anyone looking, I'll send them your way."

"That's good of you."

He nods. "We've gotta stick together, although…"

He flicks his cigarette butt to the floor and says darkly, "You touch my sister again and I'll change my mind. So, it's up to you, I make a good friend but a bastard of an enemy. This is your final warning."

He doesn't expect an answer, and I'm not prepared to offer one and as he turns and walks away, something tells me enemies it is because Devon Santiago is not the kind of man who treats his friends right and any new members he sends my way will have only one loyalty—to him.

I watch him ride off back to the pit of hell and think about Sky. He got one thing right, she is the finest woman to live around these parts and I always did love the finer things in life. Then again, I always loved a challenge, and he just threw one right at my feet.

Grabbing my keys, I don't head off into the night, I do what I've been itching to do and start walking.

Maybe I will grab that drink after all.

CHAPTER 1

SKYE

Earlier

Tonight is going to be a good one, I can feel it deep down. There's something in the air, something powerful that's going to change me forever. I can feel it. I'm sure of it, because as soon as I woke up this morning, it was with a different sort of feeling inside.

I head into the bar and see my aunt sitting on one of the stools, counting the takings from the night before.

"Hey, you should be doing that in the office, it's more secure."

She waves her hand dismissively. "We're closed and I doubt anyone would try to get inside at this early hour. Most of the people who head this way have probably only just reached their beds."

"Even so."

I reach for the ever boiling coffee pot and pour us both a mug and slide on a stool beside her.

"Do you want a hand with that?"

"Sure, you can double check it if you like."

"As if it needs double checking, I've never known you to make a mistake before."

She nods and I smile as I start counting because Aunt Rose never makes a mistake, in any part of her life. She owns this bar along with my parents, although they choose to stay away and run the same one in the next town. The Coyote bar. A chain of two and run by family. My brother Grady helps out occasionally but is more interested in running his tattoo shop on the edge of town. Three businesses that are booming thanks to all our hard work and penny pinching.

"So, Skye, tell me about the professor you have your eye on."

I smile because as soon as I think of James Adams, I can't help it.

"He may be in later, I have a good feeling about today."

"Here's hoping."

She smiles and says with curiosity, "Has he asked you on a date yet?"

"No, but he will. I get the vibes from him, you know, stolen looks and unspoken promises. I'm guessing he hasn't asked because I used to be his student; maybe he finds it weird, but there's a definite attraction, there always was."

My aunt looks worried. "Are you sure he's the one you should be concentrating on? I mean, surely if he was going to ask, he would have done so by now and I don't want you wasting your time waiting for something that's not going to happen."

A small shiver passes through me as I think about James. He was my English professor at college; handsome, clever, witty and everything I ever wanted, all rolled up into a man with the most gorgeous English accent. Who wouldn't want him? He was the object of every student's fascination, and yet there were times that our eyes used to meet across the classroom where it was just the two of us. In our own little world with the promise of unfinished business.

I used to hang back after class to ask him a question, just to be near him as I looked over his shoulder at my work on his desk. I always dressed how I thought he liked it and made sure that my makeup was hot and many times I imagined us fucking on his desk in a moment of passion that neither of us could control. Yes, James was the man I always wanted and now I'm out of college and managing a business, there will be no stopping us.

Aunt Rose sighs, "I hope it works out for you, honey, I really do because I miss a man around the place since Billy died."

I place my hand over hers and squeeze it with a reassurance that she's not on her own, but I know she feels his loss deeply.

Billy ran an MC Club, the Dragon's Ruin, and was gunned down inside his clubhouse. Nobody knows why, and his sons were hell bent on revenge. One of them, Sawyer, is ok. I can just about tolerate him because he's been so sweet to my aunt but ... I shiver as I think of his brother, Slade Channing. I've heard some weird shit about that guy and none of it good, unless you count the fact he's supposed to be the king of orgasms around these parts. Not that I'd know much about that because I've been saving myself for James.

No, I'm no biker whore and never will be. I want more and I want it with James.

We finish up and I collect the cash to store in the safe before I head to the bank later on today.

Aunt Rose looks weary and I know she was up early because she's finding it really hard to sleep, so I say gently, "Hey why don't you grab some sleep, I can sort the bar out, it looks as if you've done most of it, anyway."

She smiles sadly and nods. "Thanks, I think I'll just head out the back and take a nap. Call me before we open."

As I watch her go, I feel the pain that goes with knowing someone you love is hurting inside and there is absolutely nothing you can do about it. I'm not sure there's even an answer to it except time passing because I'm guessing if you love someone as hard as they did, it must be the cruelest of blows to live without them.

I just hope that when I meet my soul mate like Rose did Billy, we are half as much in love as they were.

∼

I LOVE WORKING in the bar but it can be tiring and yet there aren't that many opportunities around these parts. Most of the guys either head out of town, the decent ones anyway, and the rest join a biker gang, mainly to offer them protection because life around here can be tough. Which is why I've developed a hard outer shell because I get them all in here even though I've made it known bikers aren't welcome.

So, my heart sinks when later on this evening, several of my customers head inside looking worried and tell me one of them is currently resting against my wall outside. I know immediately who it is because he has come here every night for the past two weeks with only one thing on his mind - me.

Devon Santiago is the president of the Dark Lords MC and despite being handsome in a rough sort of way, he is definitely trouble that I don't want, or need. Every night I tell him to leave and every night he asks me on a date. Tonight, I've had enough and after the third person comes in and looks scared shitless, I head his way to warn him off - for good.

As soon as I hit the darkness, I see him. Leaning against the wall looking dark and dangerous. He sees me coming and straightens up, and I see the promise in his eyes as he directs his dark stare toward me.

"Hey, baby, did you miss me?"

I know many girls around here would give anything to be in my sneakers right now because Devin Santiago is one cool guy, with a face that wouldn't look out of place in a movie. He has dark hair, cropped close to his head and bright blue eyes that pierce your soul. His body is ripped and the leather jacket he wears gives him a sense of danger that makes most people breathless, but not me. It just makes me mad and I say angrily, "You're putting my customers off, please leave."

"I will if you'll come with me, how about it, baby, slide behind me on my bike and I'll take you on the ride of your life?"

He grins with what I'm sure he thinks is devilish charm but I shiver with revulsion, not desire and say tightly, "No thanks, some of us have work to do and even if I was killing time, I still wouldn't want to go on a ride with you, either on that machine, or off it, got it!"

A slow grin spreads across his face and I wonder if he's all there, mentally speaking. Surely, after hearing the same thing, two weeks in a row must have hit home by now. He's either deluded or can't understand why I'm not swooning right now and if I was to liken him to a character in a movie, it would be Gaston in Beauty and the Beast because quite frankly, he couldn't love himself any more if he tried.

He swaggers toward me and I'm sure he thinks that's all it will take to make me fall for his chat and so I stand hands on hips and say angrily, "Please leave before I call the cops. You have been warned."

Then I turn and head back inside before he can reach me and slam the door angrily. God forbid James turns up and leaves because of him, so I take a few deep breaths and paste a smile on my face and get back to business.

It doesn't stay there long because the next customer that heads through that door makes me even angrier.

I stare at him in shock because I never thought I'd see him again. To be honest, I hoped to never see him again because something about this man terrifies me and that's not easy to do. I swallow hard as he brings with him a sense of danger, of destiny and of something that is unpredictable and so dark I'm almost blinded.

Slade Channing. That's all I need. Billy's son and the new president of the Dragons Ruin MC. What is this, president night because I'm sure the two presidents of the local MC clubs have much better things to do than spend time in the Coyote Bar and yet, here he is.

Once again, he drags the atmosphere down to the pit of hell as my customers look around nervously. Where Devon is good looking in a movie star kind of way, Slade is so beautiful, it takes my breath away. Dark hair that touches his shoulders and those eyes. So dark they trap a woman's soul. He wears a shadow of stubble across his chin and a scar above his eye that proves beauty can be tarnished and yet not diminished in any way. A rough diamond, a god among men and a devil on earth.

Yes, Slade Channing's reputation precedes him and I do shiver this time, with a flash of unwelcome desire that could spell trouble for a 22-year virgin who is waiting for an angel, not a devil, to show her what love is.

Our eyes connect across the room and I can't look away. I hate the fact my heart is pounding and I lick my dry lips as he heads my way. My soul weeps and my libido wakes up because suddenly, I am seeing what all the fuss is about. If you could orgasm just by looking, I've just had several because there is something about a bad boy that gets a woman's pulse racing and her juices flowing and knowing how depraved this man is not putting me off him one bit.

Quickly, I remind myself that he is the last man I need in my life and conjure up images of James to wash the one of him away because I need Slade Channing in my life like a dose of the clap and that's definitely what I would get if I let the dirty bastard anywhere near me.

"Are you here to see Rose?"

I face him defiantly across the bar because if he's here for anyone, it's got to be her.

"Is she in?"

His voice is deep and husky, the sort that makes you forget your own name and keeps your attention all night. Danger, desire and depravity are wrapped in his sentences because just hearing him speak is sending a message straight to my clenched pussy. "Depends."

"On what?"

"If you're going to be nice to her."

"Nice" He cocks a brow and looks amused. "I don't do nice, darlin', haven't you heard?"

"I've heard."

I stare at him long and hard and fix a disinterested look on my face because I am definitely *not* interested in him. I think my body disagrees because it has been denied a man so long and is giving up hope. It's heard the rumors about the sex god before me and is fascinated to know what that would feel like - what *he* would feel like and I suppose if anyone's allowed one guilty pleasure in life, it's imagining what it would be like to go with this man just once.

I push the unwelcome thoughts away and snap my business head on and say briskly, "If you buy a drink, I'll see if she's free."

"Whiskey, neat."

I nod and reach for the bottle and try to ignore the man who my body appears to adore, but my head hates with a passion. It's exhausting being me sometimes, so I sigh and push the drink across and say curtly, "I'll see if she's free."

Quickly, I turn away but in doing so, see another customer has come into the bar and this time my attention is grabbed for a whole different reason.

James is here.

CHAPTER 2

SLADE

I don't know what made me come here in the first place, but now I'm here I'm regretting it. I suppose seeing Devon outside staking his claim on the fiery woman behind the bar, set me a challenge I've been thinking on for some time. I've only met Skye Slater once before, and that brief encounter made a lasting impression. The derision in her eyes, her obvious temper and her body so perfect in every way, imprinted itself on my mind and has burned so hard it's there permanently.

Now I'm here, I'm even more interested because that aggression, the hatred and the fact she obviously can't stand the sight of me, is turning me on so badly it hurts. I love an unwilling woman because I'm a bastard and she is the best example of one I think I've ever seen. Just imagining her passion being put to good use in the bedroom is making my cock throb so hard it's almost painful. She thinks I'm here to see Rose, my father's wife, she's wrong. I came here to erase a memory; to get her out of my mind and out of Devon Santiago's bed. I'm here for Skye because I decided the only way to get her out of my head is to break her.

She turns to leave, to call her aunt, but something makes her stop and look to the door. Her face changes and the hard, angry look is replaced by one that takes my breath away. Her eyes shine and she bites her bottom lip nervously that sends the blood rushing straight to my already rock-hard cock, and she pulls herself up to her full height and coughs nervously, before fixing a blinding smile on her face and saying, "Mr. Adams, it's so good to see you."

There is no aggression in her voice or manner for whoever this Mr. Adams is, and I physically ache to turn around and see for myself the man who has melted the ice maiden.

She's almost forgotten I'm here as she heads to the other end of the bar and says almost breathlessly, "What can I get you, sir?"

I almost come on the spot just hearing her speak and using my preferred form of address. Just picturing her tied up at my feet, bound and helpless, looking at me through those gorgeous blue eyes, saying that same sentence to me, makes up my mind in an instant. She's mine and she doesn't even know it yet.

The voice that answers her tells me he's not from around here, hell, not even from the same country and I suppose it's the accent that attracts but as I sneak a look, I see a man who is dressed well, clean cut and dripping respectability, looking at her with a fondness that shows they have history.

I can't help but listen as he says softly, "How are you keeping, Skye?"

"Fine thank you, sir. We don't see you in here much, are you meeting someone?" I hear the hope in her voice and I'm guessing if his date rocked up now she would be destroyed, but I don't miss the soft way he answers her, "No, I'm on my own."

There is some kind of promise in that sentence and for a

moment they just stare at each other and my anger is growing by the second.

I slam the glass down on the counter which has the desired effect as Skye looks up and says quickly, "Sorry, I'll be right back."

I watch her tight ass sway toward the door at the rear of the bar and know she's heading off to find her aunt. It suits me to have a reason to be here because unlike Devon, I can hide behind it; use it in my pursuit of the woman who is obviously lusting after the man beside me.

We are opposites; I am dark, where he is light. There is nothing bad about this man, which makes me wonder what his dirty little secret is because as sure as I'm going to fuck Skye Slater, that guy has a secret that I'm going to make my top priority in finding.

"Rose says to go through."

I look up and see the annoyed look of a woman who probably wanted Rose to tell me to go to Hell, so I nod and push past her without another word.

Skye has angered me a little. Just seeing her obvious desire for the guy to my right has brought out feelings I never associated with me. I'm jealous. In fact, I'm struggling to remove my head from that situation and concentrate on the one I'm in now.

As I knock on the door, I'm not sure what I'm even going to say but as she calls me in, I don't need an opener because she is standing and just smiles with a dignity that makes me like her, despite myself.

"I'm pleased to see you, Slade; surprised but pleased none the less."

"Why are you surprised?"

My voice betrays my emotions and sounds cold and hard in the room, and she shrugs. "I figured you wouldn't want to see me again after you discovered your brother knew about Billy and me, but we kept it from you."

"He had his reasons."

She nods and waves toward a chair opposite hers. "Take a seat, I'm happy to answer any questions you may have."

I sit down and feel a little strange if I'm honest. It's not like me to have meaningful conversations and especially with a woman, one that is officially my step mother but a stranger to me.

When Billy married Rose, it was in secret. A secret I only found out three months after he died. I do have questions and as she pours me a drink, I find myself liking the woman as she hands me a double whiskey and smiles.

"Always better to purge the soul on a whiskey, wouldn't you agree?"

I nod and as she leans back and takes a slug of her own, my impression changes again. Rose is struggling. Like me, she's hurting and if we have anything in common, it's that.

"How long were you together?"

My first question makes it out of my mouth, and I'm almost as surprised as she is. "Three years."

She smiles at my shock and says wistfully. "We'd known each other all through school, then as you know, I married his friend Buck. When your mother died, Billy came calling a lot more. Buck had been gone a while and Billy liked coming here."

I know why because living at the Castle is not easy and looking around, I see a warm and cozy home with a fine woman to sound off to. Her smile fascinates me as she opens up a little.

"I loved Billy. It was a different kind of love than my first husband. I think Billy was my soul mate. We had gone past the need for constant sex and craved companionship more."

She laughs and I note the sudden blush to her cheeks as

she shakes herself. "It was more than just physical with Billy and me. It was a meeting of souls and I feel as if mine died with him that day. It's hard to carry on as if there's not a huge gaping wound inside me that is slowly killing me."

"It will pass." I sound like a bastard because even though she is opening up to me, I have just dismissed it out of hand. I didn't mean to be so cruel and as she looks a little shaken, I say coolly, "You see, I felt the same when my mom died."

I almost break because god knows why I brought that subject up. It's one I protect and keep inside for my information only. Losing mom devastated me and so I understand a little of Roses' pain. Maybe I have the right to comment because I lost the only woman I have ever loved.

As if she understands, Rose nods. "I know you're right; it will just take time. Billy told me it wasn't easy when Saskia died, for all of you. We spoke about it a lot because I had lost Buck and knew something of the pain death leaves on the living."

"Did you know her?"

I wonder if Rose knew my mom and she nods. "Yes, I knew her, Slade. She was a strong woman, full of grit and determination. She was a lot like you, really; she gave nothing away and to an outsider, she was cool, aloof and troubled."

I stare at her sharply, but she is just stating the obvious. I know I'm like my mom, so I just shrug. "It's better that way."

I'm surprised when she reaches out and takes my hand, and my first instinct is to snatch it away. I feel bad as she shakes her head and says sadly, "It's lonely shutting the world out. You should deal with your pain because it will only destroy you. I'm not pretending I know a lot on the subject but I know you're struggling and if you ever need somewhere to come - a friendly ear to talk it through, I'm here."

"I don't need anyone. I'm here for answers, that's all."

"Are you sure about that?"

"Why?" She smiles and I see a steely glint in her eye as she nods toward the bar.

"Don't hurt her."

"Who?"

"You know who I'm taking about. Skye."

"I don't think anything of her."

"That's why I'm asking, don't hurt her."

She sighs and fills her glass again and says sadly, "Skye's a dreamer; an innocent in a world she should really wise up to. She's different to most girls and is looking for sunshine and rainbows. She doesn't want the darkness and the shadows and is drawn to the light. If you have designs on my niece and I wouldn't blame you if you did, back away now because she's not like the other girls you usually meet."

Her expression makes me do something I've never done before, and that shocks me more than anything. She looks so worried it's like a bullet to my heart. I don't want to upset Rose. I'm not sure why, but I don't want to be the man responsible for dealing her more shit than she's able to stand. I can tell her niece is all she's got left and no doubt like a daughter to her. It would be so easy to ruin Skye; to break her and move on to the next. But knowing what that would do to this woman, who my father loved so much he kept her a secret out of fear for her safety because of the shit we deal with every day, I do something I never have before. I back off.

An understanding passes between us and as she refills my glass, she smiles. "Stay a while, Slade. It would be good to talk to someone about Billy; someone who knows him better than I did. I want you to fill in the gaps because then it will be like having him back with me. Would you do that —for me?"

I nod, a ball of emotion weighing deep inside me. She's

right, it will be good to talk about my father because that is something my family rarely do—talk. We bottle it up and let it out in the wrong kind of ways. Maybe this is why I needed to come here tonight, and so I raise my glass and say with some emotion. "To Billy."

CHAPTER 3

SKYE

He's here. I can't believe that James is here, sitting at my bar, looking at me with interest. He watches me as I work and I'm ashamed to admit I put a show on for him alone. I'm used to men ogling my body, but I want him to see just what could be his if he gave us a chance. Occasionally, I head over and refill his glass and don't miss the spark of lust in his eyes when his fingers brush against mine as I hand him the drink.

By the time I close up, the tension is at breaking point and as the last customer leaves, he says regretfully, "I should go."

"Don't."

I'm not sure why but I feel ashamed for voicing something that could make me regret it and yet he looks at me and says softly, "Why?"

"Um, stay for a drink - with me. It would be good to catch up."

He nods toward a booth in the corner. "I'll wait there."

My heart is pounding as I reach up and grab a couple of glasses and a bottle of wine that's half empty. Then I head his way and love the way his eyes linger on my body and scorch my soul as his meaning is clear. He wants me.

I slide in beside him and my leg touches his, making me melt inside with a burst of longing that has been there for some time.

"So, here we are."

He stares at me with a long, lazy look and I lick my lips and say softly, "Yes, here we are."

"You." We both speak at the same time and laugh and he says, "After you."

I giggle a little self-consciously. "This is strange, isn't it? I feel a little shy around you."

To my surprise, he reaches out and pushes my hair back from my eyes and whispers, "I came looking for you tonight."

"Me." I'm almost shivering with need as he traces a path down my cheek and pulls my head closer. His lips are an inch away from mine and he whispers, "I always felt a connection with you, Skye. I know you felt it too, the looks, the after-class meetings, the yearning for something that was forbidden but bigger than both of us."

"Yes." My voice is breathless and sounds husky, and he groans. "I want you, Skye. I've always wanted you; do you feel the same?"

"I do." His lips crush mine in a show of passion that I am eager to enjoy. His tongue twists mine in a death grip as he ravages my lips, and then he presses in hard against me and groans. "So, beautiful, so sexy and so edible."

His hand runs around my waist and pulls me closer and his other hand reaches under my top and palms my breast, tweaking my nipple so hard a sudden burst of pain hits me. I push away the strange feeling of not being completely comfortable with this because this is James Adams, the professor that has haunted my dreams for longer than I can remember. I have dreamed of this moment and now it's happening.

My heart beats so fast I almost pass out as he dips his hand under my skirt and I feel him push my panties aside. He groans as his finger dips inside the wet trail that is proving how much I want him, and I stiffen as I feel his fingers in a place not many have been before. His kisses are hard and demanding and I do everything in my power to keep up. I can't let him down; I must prove to him that I am everything he needs because after all, I have been saving myself for him and I need to make this count.

So, I don't object when he removes my top and my skirt soon follows. I gasp as he unhooks my bra and my breasts spring free and I try to love the fact he feasts on them, sucking, licking and biting until I squirm because this is nothing like I thought it would be.

He unzips his pants and takes my hand and pushes it inside, and I feel his hard shaft throbbing in my hands. He growls, "Feel what you do to me, Skye. See how hard I am for you. Do you want it, do you want me because I want you so badly?"

"Yes," The words leave my lips before I have time to think about this. Of course, I want him, I always have, and now my dreams are about to become a reality. This is it, the moment I have been waiting for. Protecting my innocence for the man I love and as he shrugs his pants down and pulls me onto his lap, I say fearfully, "Maybe we should stop for a moment."

He tears a condom open with his teeth and smiles. "Don't be afraid. This had been building for months, years even. Don't deny us this moment because god knows I have been dreaming of you riding my cock since the day we met."

He fists my hair and I suppose it's the passion in him that makes it hurt a little and he groans. "Come on baby, don't deny me something I've wanted more than air. I know you feel it too. Let me fuck you, I know you want this."

How can I argue with that, I do? I've wanted this for so long, I can't quite believe it's happening now. I can't ruin this moment and so I nod, even though I never expected it to be this way. "Ok."

With a growl, he sheaths his cock and before I know what's happening, he lifts my hips and rams me down hard on his rock-hard cock. The pain blinds me to anything as I feel him take my virtue in one brutal moment of pain. I gasp as he growls, "Fuck me, you're a virgin."

I feel so ashamed and he continues to pump inside me with an excitement that wasn't there before. "You feel so good, so tight, so new."

It's hurting so much I want to scream out but know if I did my aunt would come running and I just hope she's had enough whiskey to send her into a deep sleep because the thought of her catching me in this position, makes my heart break.

James is so turned on he seems to have forgotten I'm here at all as he pounds me ruthlessly. Then as he takes my breast in his mouth, he bites so hard I cry out. He takes that as a sign of encouragement and goes harder, faster and deeper, and I think the pain will never end. I feel so sore and well, dirty and it's nothing like I thought it would be and as he stills and then roars, I know he's reached some kind of climax that fills me with relief. It's over.

It feels a little awkward as I lie against him, still impaled on his cock, and I'm not sure what I should do right now. Do we cuddle, whisper words of love of how amazing that was, what the hell happens now?

He shifts and then lifts me off and laughs softly, "That was so good, thanks baby."

I feel a physical pain between my legs and stare in horror

at the blood coating my thighs and his dick. He laughs and winks. "I never dared hoped you were a virgin. It felt good though."

"Um, thanks."

I feel mortified as I try to pull on my panties and feel the embarrassment burning me up as he looks at his watch. "Wow, is that the time? I should be heading home."

"Will I see you tomorrow?" I hate the way my voice sounds so needy, and he shrugs, "I'm not sure, I have a lot of work to do and should really get down to it."

"When then?"

He looks a little irritated and sighs heavily. "Listen, Skye, I understand that you probably want hearts and roses after giving me your virginity, I get that, so I'll be gentle with you. I'm not really the settling down kind, but if you like I'll make an exception with you."

For some reason I feel a surge of hope at his words despite his cool manner and he pulls me to my feet and kisses me softly on the lips. "I'll call you; maybe we can meet up next week and do this again. You will probably need that time to recover, anyway. Just…"

He breaks off and sighs. "Just don't expect more from this than it is. I like you, Skye, I really do, but I'm not looking for anything outside of a hook up from time to time. Maybe one night we can grab a meal out, but I'm not really the dating kind. Sorry, but I never pretended otherwise."

"Then why did you come here, was it just for—that?"

I feel sick as he shrugs. "Like I said before, I knew we had unfinished business and I thought you knew the score. I've never had a problem before, although I always wait until they aren't my students anymore. I have my principles."

"Get out."

My voice is laced with steel as my world comes crashing

down, and he shakes his head as if in disappointment. "Hey, you don't mean that."

"I said get out and the only reason I'm not shouting right now, is so I don't wake my aunt. So, take your disgusting principles and shove them so far up your ass you'll choke on them and never, I repeat never, come to this bar again, or I'll report you so darned quickly to the college for leading your students on. Now fuck off, I never want to see you again."

Luckily for him, he says nothing and just leaves as quickly as he can and as I slam the door shut behind him and move the bolt in place, I feel as if my soul has left my body because I couldn't feel more dirty, more degraded or emptier if I tried.

CHAPTER 4

SLADE

I'm not sure what woke me, but as I open my eyes, I struggle to remember where I am. Then it all comes flooding back as I remember drinking and talking with Rose until past midnight before she hauled herself off to bed, telling me to sleep off the alcohol on the couch.

Thinking of Rose makes me smile inside. She was a nice surprise - unexpected and a woman I enjoyed spending time with. She told me stories of my father that even had me smiling, and I love the way she drank me under the table. Rose is a hard woman, and who wouldn't respect that?

Groaning, I ease off the small couch and stretch my limbs. My head is pounding, but I feel sober enough to ride home, even though I probably shouldn't. I can't stay here though. Just picturing the disapproval on Skye's face is enough to send me heading for the door; why that bothers me I don't know, but I made a promise to Rose last night, leave her niece alone. If I want to come back and spend some time with Rose, hear more stories and escape from the Dragons for a while, I need to keep my promise.

It occurs to me as I head out the way I came in, that I'm in a strange position. Passing up the chance of a hot girl because an old lady asked me to.

As I push open the door to the bar, it strikes me how strange this place is when it's empty with no customers. It's in darkness but the moon is still out and its beams touch parts of the room, highlighting the way out.

I move quietly and then a sound stops me in my tracks and I hear it again. A gentle sob coming from somewhere across the room and I move in its direction.

I can just make a hunched figure clutching her knees and rocking on the seat in a booth and recognize her immediately.

She doesn't appear to have noticed me, so I say gently so as not to scare her, "Are you ok, darlin'?"

She looks up and the haunted eyes that stare at me make something snap inside and I crouch down beside her and say in a whisper, "Are you hurt?"

She looks so sad, so destroyed, I can only think that someone has died and her lower lip trembles as she shakes her head. "Not really."

I'm in alien territory and don't know what the fuck to do now and just say weakly, "Shall I fetch your aunt?"

"NO!" The panic in her eyes stops me and I say gently, "Can I fetch you anything, a blanket, a hot drink, a whiskey?"

I smile hoping to put her at ease and she shakes her head and whispers, "I'm so stupid, Slade."

The fact she's remembered who I am is a relief because from the look on her face, she's not really here at all, mentally that is and I see her teeth chatter and the goosebumps on her arms and realize she's freezing. Quickly, I remove my leather jacket and place it around her and she looks at me gratefully and whispers, "Thank you."

I'm so out of my comfort zone, but I can't leave her and

just head to the bar and flick the coffee machine on. "I'll fetch you a hot drink, you're cold."

I'm not sure if she even heard me and just stares into the darkness with a look of utter devastation on her face. As I make the drinks, I think hard and the only thing I can think of is that fucker she liked, hurt her in some way. Maybe he wasn't interested and shattered her dreams. Maybe he did meet someone else, and she's finding it hard to deal with. I can't think of any other reason, unless that idiot Devon came back and tried something. As I think about that, the blood freezes in my veins as I picture him anywhere near her.

Quickly, I grab a couple of coffees because I could sure use one myself and sit beside her and say gently, "Here, you need this."

Her fingers wrap around the mug and she nods. "Thanks."

As we sit side by side, it feels awkward as fuck. I'm not this man, the concerned Samaritan who looks after a woman in crisis. Hell, I normally cause the crisis and I find I have no words to use for the situation I'm in and then she says, "Have you ever done something you regretted the moment you started."

"Yes." I can actually think of several things, most of what I do I know will end in regrets but I can't imagine what she's done that's so bad.

"How do you deal with it?"

"I don't."

I shrug and take a sip of my drink and lean back. "I just carry on and hope the next thing I do won't make me feel like shit. It always does though."

I laugh and add. "You see, one thing I've learned is that I know shit about everything and just do what seems right at the time."

"I never have."

"Then what's your problem?"

"I broke that rule tonight."

"Do you wanna talk about it?" I'm not sure I even want to know, but she is so broken I'm curious to find out.

"I'm not sure."

She seems so wrapped up in shadows, I have a strange feeling inside of wanting to help, so I say in as soft a voice as I can, "It helps to talk."

"Does it? Somehow I don't have you down as the talking kind."

She seems to shake herself and drains the mug and appears to gather her defenses around her and says in a stronger voice, "Anyway, what are you doing here, I thought you left hours ago?"

"You were wrong."

"And Rose?"

"Drank me under the table, I expect she's sleeping it off right now."

For the first time Skye laughs softly and I don't know why I love the sound of it so much, but I do.

"Well, I should be getting to bed, I'll see you out."

She waits for me to stand and then as she follows me, says softly, "Here, this is yours, I believe."

I turn and she hands me my leather jacket with the club emblem emblazoned on the back and something inside me loves seeing her in it. I've never given a woman my jacket before, and I'm liking the view. Skye Slater is an impressive one and I am struggling to tear my eyes from the image before me.

She thrusts it to me and as my hands close around it, she says firmly, "Now get the hell out of my bar, biker." She smiles to take the sting from her words and then says softly, "Thank you."

As she holds open the door and the icy blast of air from

outside reminds me how early this is, I wrap my jacket around me and nod. "Pleasure, darlin'."

I turn to leave, but something catches my attention as the door closes and for a moment I freeze on the spot. The door closes and I hear the bolt drag across and yet I still stand staring at the wood not quite understanding the sudden rage that is consuming me right now because what I saw made the puzzle fit and I'm not sure I can deal with the picture. There was blood staining Skye's clothes which told me exactly what she regretted and now I'm so angry I have only one thing on my mind. Revenge.

CHAPTER 5

SKYE

I can't accept what happened last night. When Slade left, I dragged myself to the shower and tried so hard to clean away the imprint of James from my body. The blood sickened me and the pain where he ripped my virginity from me in a selfish act of pleasure, reminds me what a fool I was.

No matter how hard I scrubbed, I couldn't remove his touch, and it's as if he has burned every part of me, inside and out.

I go through the motions, but I'm dying inside. I'm such a fool. I never saw what he was really after. I thought he loved me, which shows just what an idiot I am. He only wanted another tick on his to do list and by the sounds of it, it's a long one.

I have graduated from the school of James Adams and now it's up to me to take the lesson and learn from it.

Aunt Rose keeps looking at me as if she knows something is up, and I try so hard to push away the pain and carry on as if nothing happened.

As we clean the bar, she says with interest. "So, how are things with the professor, I heard he was in last night?"

"I'm not sure I like him anymore."

I turn away and casually mop the bar and she says in shock, "Since when."

"Last night, actually. He came in and I didn't have that same spark I always had and to be honest, I don't know what I ever saw in him."

My Aunt is no fool and I can sense something is on her mind and after an awkward few minutes, I sigh and put down my bar cloth. "Ok, what is it?"

"Slade."

"What about him?"

"Did he try anything last night?"

"No, of course not, anyway, he was with you, maybe I should ask you the same question."

She laughs softly and looks relieved. "Good, it seems my lecture worked."

"What lecture?"

"I told him to leave you alone, you deserve more, like that professor you're so keen on. Not a bad boy biker who has a reputation with women and not a good one, I might add."

"Well, you can rest easy because nothing happened with Slade last night, period. Anyway, he's never shown any interest in me, so you've got it wrong."

"Have I?"

Aunt Rose heads off to the kitchen before I can answer, which leaves me alone with my thoughts about the surly biker.

He surprised me last night. I never intended on talking to him, especially not after what happened, and yet not once did he hit on me. I doubt he's even interested because I'm certainly not, but it felt nice having someone to talk to, even though he didn't know what the hell I was doing rocking in the shadows like a mad woman. I'm not sure why he was my first thought when I woke, probably because he was the last person I saw last night, although maybe my brain was replacing a traumatic experience with something else to think about because I just can't deal with what I did last night.

The day stretches interminably, and it doesn't help that I feel so sore between my legs and inside it feels as if I've been attacked with sandpaper. I am trying so hard to forget what I did, what I let happen because I'm in no doubt, I wanted it. Be careful what you wish for, they say, that's true enough and as the day goes on, I get more and more desperate as I see loving couples walking in, holding hands. Old married couples, content and knowing they have each other. Flirtatious looks from guys who I know are married and ones that I wouldn't go near if you paid me to.

Then Devon rocks up and I feel so weary knowing I must send him away again. This is my life, an endless repetition of the same, and for what? Broken dreams and shattered promises. Real life is brutal, and I was a fool thinking otherwise.

Once again, I head outside to find Devon leaning on the wall and his eyes glitter as I walk toward him, with none of the usual fire reserved for him.

"Hey, baby."

"Hey."

I look at him through new eyes and realize just how handsome he is, in a dark kind of way.

"You ready for that ride, baby?"

As I look at him, I see a man whose intent is right out there for anyone to see. I know what he wants. He doesn't disguise it with smoke and mirrors. Maybe I should take him up on his offer. Go for that ride and see what all the fuss is about. I hear the whispers around town. He's hot property and most would think me a fool to pass up this opportunity. One thing's for sure, I need to harden my heart against love because look where that got me. I need to be harder, sharper and in charge of my life. Not let another man ruin me and break my heart so cruelly.

"What did you have in mind?"

If he's surprised, he doesn't show it and just moves closer and I breathe in the scent of cigarettes and sexual intent.

"Whatever you like, baby, I'm all yours."

Suddenly, I'm weary. It's so hard fighting him off, and for what? I know what he wants, what they all want, and yet I'm in no position to play the game. I know nothing and all the time I hide behind my bar, I'm not learning how to protect myself. Looking at Devon makes me realize I'm not ready. I can't handle someone like him, I'm too innocent. As I look into his eyes, he steps forward a little and our lips briefly touch. I almost think he's going to kiss me and then he whispers, "I've been waiting for you a long time, baby. When do you get the night off?"

"I don't."

"Then make the time because you and me, it's gonna happen and once you've had a taste of me, you are never gonna want to let me go."

He steps back and says firmly, "Arrange the time and let me know when. I'll pick you up and prepare to be some time."

He heads to his bike and I stand and watch him head off in a blaze of fumes and promises.

What the fuck have I just agreed to?

It bothers me for the rest of the night. I can't go with him, he's a player - a man, not a boy. Maybe I need someone like him, someone to show me how to be a woman because last night only showed me one thing. I know nothing.

As I go through the motions of running the bar, a sudden idea hits me that makes me wonder if I've lost my mind. I push it away but it keeps on coming back and by the end of the night, I know exactly what I have to do.

CHAPTER 6

SLADE

I can't shake what I saw last night and have spent the whole day finding out everything I can about Professor Adams. Marina thought I'd gone mad when I told her to spread the word and dig up shit on the teacher.

I'm so angry I can't function properly because what I saw staining Skye's legs will haunt me to my dying day. The fact I've been responsible for much worse in my time doesn't eve occur to me because I'm that deluded. If I do it, it's in the name of pleasure, the woman's pleasure and the fact they keep on coming back for more, shows me I'm doing something right, but Skye, she looked as if she had just met the devil and was burning up in hell. So much for respectability, turns out the devil changes his clothes from time to time.

I know I'm being a bastard, but I can't help it. Lack of sleep, too much whiskey, and the encounter with Skye has wrapped me in impatience and irritation. Whatever happens, I will make him pay, I'm just not sure how yet. The fact it's not even my problem doesn't occur to me because now I'm seeing the black mist of revenge instead of reasoning and like

I said to Skye, I don't think and just deal with shit as it happens.

Mid-morning and I'm starving, so I call through to the bar and Ruby answers. "I need some food, darlin', maybe a burger and fries, anything filling."

"Sure. I'll be right there."

As I replace the phone, I think about how things have changed around here in a short space of time. When Sawyer left and Axel took off on a road trip, it left me to deal with the fall out of finding Billy's killer and what happened as a result. This place is unrecognizable from what it was then because with Marina's help, we have cleaned up our act and now everyone here is treated with respect. Just thinking of how low we sank as a club makes me ashamed, and as Ruby heads inside with my meal, I smile and say gratefully, "Thanks, darlin'."

"No problem."

She turns to go and as I reach for the plate, she says as an aside, "I'm not sure if you're interested but a car just pulled up outside. There's a pretty hot girl inside and I'm not sure of her reception because a few of the Dragons are hanging outside. Just letting you know."

She turns to go and I shrug and reach for my food because that's the only thing on my mind right now.

As I do, I flick on the CCTV to take a look and what I see has me dropping the burger like it's a bomb and heading out as fast as my legs will take me.

What the… The first thing I see are two of my men cornering the girl and by the looks of things, they've learned shit about how we treat our visitors now and I shout, "Fuck off inside, both of you."

"They turn and just the look on my face is enough to have them backing off and heading inside without a backward glance.

My chest heaves as I see Skye looking like a fragile butterfly caught in a web, and her heightened color tells me those bastards were coming on to her. The relief on her face as she sees me is a strange one, because women don't see me as their knight in shining armor. I'm usually the one they try to avoid at all costs because there is not a bigger bastard than me around these parts.

I head across and note she is nervous, which immediately puts me on edge.

"Skye."

I nod and she smiles and bites her lip nervously. "Hi, Slade."

She looks around her with wide eyes because for those who don't know what goes on inside an MC club, the stories they hear create a morbid fascination with the place.

"What can I do for you?"

I'm abrupt and to the point because I need her to leave and fast. Not because of my men, because of me. The promise I made to Rose is coming back to bite me because I have never met such a desirable woman as Skye Slater.

"Um, have you got a moment?"

I'm not sure why she's so nervous and I'd be lying if I said I knew why she was here at all, so I nod. "Sure, follow me."

We head inside and I take her straight to my office because the less she sees of this place, the better. Women like Skye don't belong inside the Castle, they wouldn't last five minutes here and knowing how innocent she is, I don't want to add to the trauma she obviously experienced yesterday.

Apparently, I grew a sense of responsibility last night because ordinarily, I would be hitting on her right now, but I respect Rose and don't want to back down on my word.

As soon as we reach my office, I nod to the chair opposite my desk. "Can I get you a drink, something to eat maybe?"

My food is tormenting me from the desk and Skye

notices and smiles. "I'm interrupting your lunch, please go ahead and finish, I can talk while you eat."

"Sure you don't want some?"

"It's fine, I've eaten."

She looks nervous and plays with her fingers as she appears to be summoning up some courage from deep inside, and as I chew on my burger, I look at her through hooded eyes. I know I'm intimidating, hell I get off on it and this is no exception. It's like the spider and the fly, and this time I'm not allowed to eat my victim.

"So," she laughs nervously. "You're probably wondering why I'm here."

I just nod and she colors up a little and takes a deep breath. "You see, well, I've got a favor to ask you and it's a little strange, probably not morally right, but I can't think of anyone else to ask."

"Is it about last night?"

"Sort of."

"Go on."

I carry on eating and she stutters a little. "It's just that, well, um, oh god I don't know how to say this, I mean, what will you think? To be honest, I nearly didn't come and now I'm here I'm not sure it's such a good idea. You see, well, oh my, this is so embarrassing, maybe I shouldn't but I really need to ask…"

I reach out and grab hold of her fingers that are working themselves in knots and say gently, "Relax, darlin', you can ask me anything."

"Oh, ok, well, here goes and just for the record, I won't be offended if you say no, or anything but would you, um, what I mean to say is, oh god, I don't know if can."

If I wasn't so turned on by this woman, watching her almost faint with nerves, I keep on picturing her on her knees naked and begging me for something different. I blink twice to keep my head in business and wonder if she wants me to take someone out; if it's the teacher, I'd do it for free - bastard.

"The thing is, Slade, I want to ask if you'll…"

"What darlin'?"

"Teach me sex."

CHAPTER 7

SKYE

Oh my god, I actually said the words. I can't believe it, what was I thinking? I almost can't look because for some reason, Slade blinds me to common sense. I made the decision last night after agreeing to go out with Devon. I need to get experience and fast, and I can't think of a better man for the job, if his reputation is anything to go by. I need to make up for lost time and he will be the perfect teacher. Cold, unfeeling and clinical. No emotion and no ties. At the end of it we can walk away; it had to be him.

The look on his face makes me squirm with embarrassment as he holds his burger in mid-air and looks as if I just killed his cat.

"What did you say?" His tone is low and ominous, and I laugh nervously. "Teach me, um, sex. I'm sorry to ask, but I didn't know who else to turn to. I'm afraid, last night I realized just how much I have to learn and rather than repeat the experience, I want to be prepared next time."

He puts down his food and just stares at me through narrowed eyes and I feel my heart pounding out of control. Then he says bluntly, "No."

I wasn't expecting that, and the shock must show on my face because he sighs heavily. "I made a promise to your aunt, I won't pursue you and if she knew I was fucking you, she would have a heart attack, so, no, I will not teach you and what I want to know more than anything, is why the fuck you're asking?"

He looks so angry and I suppose, after my experience last night, I feel a bad taste of rejection and stand. "It's fine, I'm sorry to have troubled you. I'll just ask Devon instead."

I turn away and in two steps he's at the door blocking my exit.

"You will not ask Devon, I forbid it."

"You can't tell me what to do."

"Yes, I can."

"No, you can't."

I make to push him away and he grabs my wrists and pulls them behind my back and spins me around, so my back is against his infernally hard chest. He leans close and whispers in a voice laced with dangerous intent, "You want to know about sex, and I want to know why? If you want my help you need to tell me every reason why you're asking and then, only then, will I consider your request."

For some reason, his closeness is doing something strange to me inside. Maybe it's the proximity, maybe it's the subject matter, or maybe because he is so darned hot my body is struggling to maintain distance and he appears in no hurry to release me. His breath is hot on my neck and his voice husky as he drawls, "You come here and ask me for something no respectable girl would ever say. You walked into the pit of hell and offered your soul to the devil. Then you dared to play me off against my rival and expect to leave with no harm done. Well, bad luck, darlin' because I don't play by the rules."

His hand wraps around my throat and pushes up against

it hard and I feel the pressure as he growls, "Do you like to feel the pain, to be tested beyond your limits and taken to the edge of darkness? Would you be willing to fall into the pit of hell with me and do things you wouldn't even think about? Would you take your body to the edge of sanity and trust me not to let you fall into madness, because baby, that's what I will teach you? If you want a crash course in fucking, I can let you loose in my bar and there are twenty Dragons who would only be too happy to oblige. So, I'll ask you again, why do you want to learn about sex?"

There is something so intimate about the way he is holding me. Just feeling him so close is making my breathing irregular and I can't even remember my own name. I am physically aching for him to touch me, it's as if I'm on the edge and need him to break my fall and lean against. I have never wanted anyone to touch me as much as I do him and just thinking of what I've asked him to do, is making me weak with desire. Is this what they talk about? That feeling of wanting someone so badly you will do anything because after my experience last night, I'm ready to dance with the devil himself to purge the memory of when my virginity was so cruelly given away like a cheap whore.

My voice shakes as I whisper, "My old teacher came to the bar last night and I let him fuck me when the bar closed."

My voice shakes as I say bitterly, "I was saving it for him anyway, but I thought it would be different. I thought he really liked me and, well, could fall in love with me. I went too far and agreed to something I was not prepared for. I thought once we… you know, had sex, it would make us a couple. You see, that's how naïve I am, because as it turns out, he was only after one thing and couldn't believe his luck when he found out my secret."

The tears slide down my face as my voice breaks. "It hurt, Slade. It was the most brutal experience of my life and I wanted him to stop. Don't get me wrong, at no point did I ask him to. I thought that was what sex was. I never imagined it could hurt so bad and then when he finished, he pushed me aside and made to leave. When I asked him when I'd see him again, he was so cold."

I sob as the hurt comes back to bite me and say with tears lacing my voice, "He used me. He told me we could hook up next week, but that's all it would be. He doesn't date, and he wasn't interested in me in that way. So, now you know."

"I know nothing."

His voice is so close to my ear, husky and laced with venom. "Why do you want to learn, so you can make it better for him next time?"

"NO!" I struggle against him and say with horror. "I never want to see the bastard again. I told him when I threw him out, but when Devon came calling again today, I decided I should harden up and get some experience. I can't keep on waiting for Prince Charming, so I need a crash course and fast."

"For Devon's benefit?" His voice holds a murderous rage and I bite my lip so hard; I taste blood.

"No." I whisper it softly. "For me. I heard sex was a wonderful experience, something magical and earth shattering. I didn't have that experience. I want to know how good it can be, and I need someone who doesn't want any more from me. Someone who will walk away and not care because I can't let emotion into this. It's a sexual project of the most depraved kind and designed to arm me with the necessary skills so I never repeat what happened last night."

For a moment, there's silence and then he releases me and I stumble forward a little.

As I turn to face him, I see a storm in his eyes as he growls, "Tomorrow, same time, same place. Meet me here and tell your aunt you're heading off for a few days with friends. Nobody must know, or ever know. It's a business deal with no emotion involved. You will do everything I tell you, with no exception. You will not question me, argue, or even speak if I say so and you will learn what you need to know. Under no circumstances are you to mention this to your aunt or anyone, do I make myself clear?"

"Yes." I almost can't look at him because I can't believe he agreed. It's really going to happen, Slade Channing has agreed to teach me what I want and now I've set the wheels in motion, I'm not sure I have all my sanity.

He looks at me with a hard stare and I drown in the deep pools of darkness in his eyes and stutter, "What do you want in return, you said it was a business transaction?"

He just grins wickedly. "I'll tell you when I figure that out. For now, you will owe me and when I come calling for payment, you had better pay up in full."

He stands aside and opens the door. "You have twenty-four hours cooling-off period. If you change your mind, we will never revisit this conversation. If you want to go ahead, pack for an overnight stay, you won't need much."

"Where…"

"Twenty-four hours, Skye, you may go."

I almost can't look at him as I stumble from his office like a deer caught in a hunter's sight. Twenty-four hours and I'll be his. God help me.

CHAPTER 8

SLADE

Well, I wasn't expecting that. I think I can count on one hand the number of times in my life I've been shocked but none of them shocked me as much as Skye just did. Teach her sex. What the fuck?

The fact I want her so badly doesn't come into it. She is easily the hottest girl around and I would be a fool to refuse. But Rose. I made a promise and I don't want to be that guy who breaks them, especially when I respect Billy's wife so much.

But I couldn't say no. She was going to ask Devon and just the thought of his hands on her skin drives me insane. As soon as she mentioned his name, it was like a red flag to a bull and my decision was made before I blocked her exit.

When I held her against me, it felt like nothing I had experienced before. I wanted her so badly and yet I'm to maintain a cool distance because one thing's for sure, Skye Slater will walk away from me if she still can at the end of it. I drive women to extremes. I'm hard, rough and violent at times and then I reward them with a special kind of loving that binds their hearts to me forever. Skye won't last the night if I unleash it all on her and just thinking of cutting her soft, white flesh with my knife, to mark her as I do all my women, makes me go cold.

I'm not sure I can treat her like the rest. She's so different from the usual girls I meet. It won't sit right with me and I need to keep my distance because by the end of this she will probably hate me forever.

Somehow, I try to get my head back into club business, but it's hard. Even attending a meeting across town about setting up a motorcycle shop isn't tearing my mind from what I'll be doing this time tomorrow. Just thinking about her reasons for asking in the first place causes something to shift inside me. It made my soul weep when she asked for something that should come naturally. Skye definitely needs a different experience from my usual women, but at what cost—to me?

I call Marina to my office the minute we get back from the realtor and fill her in on my plans for the shop. She looks impressed.

"That's great, Slade, perfect in fact. Where's the property?"

"Not far from here, about five minutes away. I was hoping we could situate it here, but it's not big enough."

"What about this place, will you keep it on?"

I shrug because I'm not ready to let this place go. It's the home of the Dragon's Ruin and always will be, but I have big plans for the club and we will soon outgrow this building, so I say with a little regret, "The one not far away is much bigger. We could run the business from the workshop out the back and sell bikes out the front. The premises are large enough inside to double as offices and a club house. Security is good, and it's modern and nothing like this shit heap that needs dragging up to date. I'm guessing we would attract a lot of new members because it makes the Dark Lord's set up look outdated but it's hard, Marina."

She nods. "I know. This is the place Billy ran the Dragons from. It's too soon after his death to turn your back on it. Maybe you could keep both, use this for something else."

"Perhaps. We have enough money to keep them both, but that is all. We need to make our businesses pay more in order to expand, which is why I need a bigger set up. I could sell this and that would give us what we need, or I could rent it out, I'm not sure yet."

Marina smiles. "Listen, Slade, I'm impressed. You have done something to make your family proud, and I'm certain Billy would tell you to move with the times. Sentimentality has no place in business, and the only thing stopping you is your own memories. If it's any help, I'd sell up. Make a clean break and run the Dragons the Slade Channing way, not Billy's or Axel's. Maybe it's time to move on, put the past behind you and well, you know what I'm talking about."

She softens her voice and leans closer. "I'm not just talking about business here, honey. You need to let someone in, make a life for yourself because you can't go on hurting so badly."

I shift away and say coolly, "Maybe I like it that way. Maybe this is who I am and if anyone needs to get their head around that, it's you, Marina. I'm all about the business and not looking for anything else, so if you want to talk about the Dragons and where we go from here, fine, just keep my private life out of it."

She nods and looks down and I am so frustrated I feel like tearing off again for the longest ride to clear my head. Everything is changing and I'm not sure I'm ready for this. Then there's Skye, my attention just can't shift away from her. I should have said no, sent her on her way and not cared if she fucked every Dark Lord's biker but just thinking of her with another man, *any* other man, was like a physical pain. I know how much I want Skye Slater, but she will never know it. I will teach her what she craves and leave my heart out of it because I am not going to let her inside, despite the fact, in my heart, I know she's already there.

CHAPTER 9

SKYE

I can't believe I'm actually doing this. I think I changed my mind several times during the night. What am I thinking?

I must have a death wish or something because no sane person asks the president of the local biker club to teach them sex.

Even as the words left my lips, I cringed with embarrassment and he seemed so angry. I thought he would leap at the chance because I've heard rumors of how sex hungry bikers are. When he explained about his deal with my aunt, it knocked me sideways. I never thought of him as a man with honor before, but apparently, I was wrong.

Then, as soon as I mentioned Devon, everything changed, and I got my deal. I may regret that later because he hasn't told me what that means for me.

On the drive over, I try to change my own mind because this is madness. I'm not one to sleep around and the one time I did, it hurt so bad I would be quite happy to be celibate. But, how can I? I want to settle down, have kids and a normal life, so I need to wise up and learn something everyone but me seems to be able to do without any problems at all.

My heart thumps so hard it's almost painful as I pull into the yard at the Dragon's Ruin and see him waiting.

I swallow hard and gulp back the fear as I see him sitting astride his Harley, dressed in leather with a look I'm having trouble reading the meaning of.

Just that one look makes me squirm and I wonder when I discovered a desire for bad boys - probably the second a good one let me down and ruined every dream I ever had. Trust it to be Slade who was around to change my perception of them because he couldn't have been nicer to me if he tried.

I park up and give myself a good talking to. I asked for this. This was all my idea, so now I must see it through and hopefully, by the end of it, I will be stronger, more capable and ready to face life like an adult instead of that naïve kid who gave herself so willingly to a monster.

With a deep breath, I head across to meet the man who will change my life, or ruin me, I'm not sure which yet and it feels so weird walking toward him knowing what he is about to do - to me.

He watches me approach and I keep my expression blank to disguise how terrified I'm feeling right now.

As I reach him, he takes my bag from my hands and stows it in a compartment on his bike and wordlessly hands me a crash helmet and a leather jacket, emblazoned with a dragon. He helps me put it on and as his fingers brush against my skin, I feel a shiver of desire run through me, showing me how fucked up I am. I don't want him - not really. He is everything I *don't* want but I need his experience, his cold detachment and when this is over, I need him to stay the hell away from me - forever.

He climbs on the bike and I take a deep breath and climb

on behind him and then realize I must wrap my arms around him to hold on. Gingerly, I hold on to him lightly and he says darkly, "Last chance, darlin', back out, or hold on tight."

I say nothing and just grip him tighter and he starts the engine and growls, "Then we have a deal."

I close my eyes, glad of the protection the helmet and jacket give me as we tear out of the yard in a haze of exhaust fumes and bad decisions.

~

IT TAKES around an hour to reach a dusty track off the freeway and as we bump along it, I wonder where we're heading. It's beautiful here, almost breath-taking as we pass cedar wood trees under a bright blue sky.

We pull into a clearing at the top of a hill and I see a wooden cabin nestling on the edge of the hilltop, looking out across glorious woods and rivers. We could be anywhere; this isn't civilization, its raw nature and probably the most perfect place we could be.

He comes to a stop and as he cuts the engine, it reinforces the fact we're on our own with no other humans around because only the sound of nature makes us welcome and the eerie silence adds to the drama of the moment.

Slade grabs two bags from the containers either side of his bike and as I hand him the helmet, he locks it inside one of them.

I feel a little nervous as I stand waiting for instruction because now we're here, I'm as nervous as hell.

He ignores me completely and heads to the cabin door and takes a key from his jacket and unlocks it.

Then he beckons me to follow him, and if ever there was a moment to change my mind, it's now. What if I can't do it? What if I immediately regret my decision? I'm here in the middle of the wilderness with a predator, this may not end well.

Feeling slightly shaky on my legs, I'm not sure if it's due to the ride, the bike, or the nerves that are tearing me up inside but I follow him in and look around with surprise as he drops the bags to the floor.

As he opens windows and checks the rooms, I stand looking in awe at a pleasant cabin that appears to have everything necessary for a cozy stay. Fur rugs litter the bare wooden floorboards and a log burner stands proudly in the corner of the room. There's a comfortable couch set before it and a low table with a lamp and candle holders. There's not a lot else, but it's clean and smells ok, nothing like I expected and as Slade comes back into the room, he says gruffly, "Bedrooms through there with a small bathroom to the side. I suggest using it before we make a start."

"What, now?" I stare at him in shock because I wasn't expecting to start so soon. I'm not sure when I thought we would, but certainly not right away.

"Yes darlin', we're here for one reason only and I'm not one for polite conversation. Go into the bathroom and take a shower, you will find a robe hanging on the back of the door, that's all you'll need."

He doesn't even look at me and turns his attention to the wood burner, and I make a quick exit before he can tell how terrified I am.

Maybe I got this wrong, I'm such a fool. Now I'm here and it's about to become a reality, I'm not sure about any of it. It's so cold, so clinical, and nothing like I heard it should be. There is no romance, hell I don't even like the guy and yet I'm about to get intimate with a monster.

The bedroom is actually really pretty, which again surprises me. I suppose I thought it would be dirty and the furniture old and past it's best. But this room is lovely in so many ways. A big brass bed takes center stage, and the bedding looks crisp and clean. Soft fluffy rugs hug the floor and once again, I notice several candles waiting to be lit. The small window has a pretty blind that has been pulled down and as I open the door to the side, I see a clean modern bathroom inside with a big bath in the center. I am actually blown away by the place and wonder who owns it.

I can hear Slade moving around outside and quickly head to the bathroom and my heart sinks when I see there's no lock on the door. Maybe that's what makes me hurry and step into a shower that feels hot and calming, and I waste no time in grabbing some soap to wash my shame away.

What would my family say if they knew where I was? I'm pretty sure they would be super disappointed in me, but I need to do this. I *want* to do this and then I can take control of my life and be better for it.

As I dry off and shrug on the white fluffy robe that's hanging on the back of the door, I shiver inside. This is it; I'm really doing this and I couldn't back out now if I tried.

For a moment, I sit on the edge of the bed and try my hardest to pull some courage from somewhere but after a while, I realize the only way to face this is head on, so with a deep breath, I head out to face the consequences of my request.

~

THE ROOM HAS BEEN TRANSFORMED and I stare around at a place dressed for seduction. The fire is now roaring in the wood burner and the candles that light every surface flicker as they dance in the darkness. He has pulled every blind, cutting out the light and bringing in the darkness, and I shiver because he watches me from across the room with a look that can only mean I have a big problem.

He stands fully dressed in his black jeans and leather jacket, and the wild look in his eye should make me cower in fear. He says nothing, just stares and I feel a little uncomfortable as I wonder what to do next.

I am actually shaking as I try to look unconcerned and as if I do this sort of thing all the time and then he says roughly. "Drop the robe."

Just the thought of it sends a flush through my whole body as I contemplate standing naked before him and yet he expects it without an argument.

He stares at me with a dark look and as I hesitate, he growls, "Now."

Quickly, I drop the robe and shiver as I stand naked before him and as his eyes rake my body, I try to focus on a shadow on the ceiling and pretend he isn't here. "Kneel."

His voice is rough, short, and there is no room for argument as I drop to my knees, just grateful for an excuse to disguise at least some part of my body.

He moves and my heart rate picks up as he walks behind me and then I feel something close around my eyes. It feels soft and silky and as he ties it in place, he whispers, "I need you to relax and this will help."

Just the fact I can't see him makes it better because for some reason, I don't feel so self-conscious like this. It heightens my senses and I strain to listen for any sounds that tell me what's happening and then he whispers, "Do you trust me, Skye."

"I think so."

"You shouldn't."

His low chuckle sounds more demonic than anything, and I feel a shiver run through me as his breath fans my skin.

"I'm going to bind your wrists behind your back for no other reason than our first lesson. Relax, I'm not going to do anything to hurt you in any way. If you want me to stop, tell me. There are no code words, no rules, just us. You must promise to tell me if you're uncomfortable with anything I do because I won't know unless I hear your words."

I nod and as I feel him bind my wrists, it occurs to me that I'm not frightened at all. I do trust him, which is something I can't explain.

He says softly. "I'm going to carry you and place you on the rug by the fire and I want you to lie still and not say a word."

I nod and as his hands touch my body, I feel it respond to him almost immediately.

He smells so good, he feels so good and it feels amazing being in his arms despite the fact I'm so exposed.

The next thing I feel is the fur rug caressing my body as he lays me gently on top of it, and the warmth from the fire heats my shivering skin.

It's so nice and there's an aroma that relaxes me that must come from one of the candles and if I feel anything, it's the purest pleasure.

He places me face down with my hands bound behind me and it feels good, less exposed and nowhere near as embarrassing.

Then I sense him crouch beside me and something soft and feathery runs down my back and feels so good, I could lie here all day.

"Do you like that, Skye."

"Yes."

"Yes, sir."

"Um, yes, sir."

"Good. I'm going to tell you the rules now and I want you to listen hard."

He carries on touching my body with the feather, making me relax and he whispers, "You will address me as sir because I am your teacher. Everything I ask you to do, you will obey with no arguments. You will trust me and want to please me because if you don't, I will have to punish you, do you understand?"

"Yes, um, sir."

I'm actually not liking the punishment part and wonder what that will involve, but I'm feeling so content right now, I'll ask him about that later.

"You will wear no clothes inside this cabin except the robe I have provided. You will be available to me whenever I ask, and you will be grateful for everything I give you. At the end of our stay, you will owe me and I reserve the right to claim that at any time. You will not speak of this to anyone and we will never refer to it again. Walk away as strangers as you wished for."

For some reason, now I've relaxed, I'm craving what he has in store because I have never felt so sensual in my life. His soft voice with rough edges, the soft touch, the warmth from the fire, is sending direct messages to the part inside me that is craving some form of release. What is it, why do I want him closer, to feel his skin against mine and his lips on my body?

To my surprise, he unties my hands and massages my wrist before kissing each one softly and with care. Then he pulls me up so I'm kneeling before him and unties the blindfold and whispers, "You may put on your robe."

I'm not sure why I feel so disappointed about that and yet as he wraps it around my shoulders and ties it securely around my waist, I get the feeling I may not be able to hold up my end of the bargain because Slade Channing has just revealed a surprising side to him that I never saw coming and it's very attractive indeed.

CHAPTER 10

SLADE

Well, this is proving harder than I thought. I'm not sure what I did think, but I suppose it was to do what she asked and then walk away with a cool detachment and never speak of this again. I meant it when I said I wanted to honor my promise to Rose, but from the moment I saw her walking toward my Harley, looking so nervous, I was interested. I've given her multiple chances to back out, but she still came and with a bravery that impressed me.

When she dropped the robe, it took all my self-control not to pounce on her and tie her to my bed before fucking her senseless. I normally would, but there is something different about Skye to the women I usually fuck. She's innocent and not used to the depravity that exists in my world, and after what I saw in the bar, I will not be the man responsible for fucking her up even more than that teacher bastard.

No, Skye needs to learn the first rule about sex and that is trust and so I need to tread carefully.

She is looking at me nervously and I say gruffly, "Come and sit with me."

She seems surprised and probably wondering what I'm

playing at. Shrugging off my jacket, I take a seat before the fire and as she heads my way, say roughly. "Face the fire and kneel before me. Drop the robe."

I feel such a thrill when she does as I say because Skye is one feisty woman and having control over her like this makes me harder than I thought possible.

As she kneels before me, I take a moment to catch my breath because I need to control myself around her. She's just too delicious, too edible, and too innocent. I lower my voice and try to inject some warmth in it because I'm not one for talking and this is as alien to me as it is to her.

"I want you to relax around me. Sex is more than fucking someone, it's made up of emotions that are as important as the physical things associated with it. You're not comfortable with me, Skye, and until you are, we can't move on."

She shivers a little and I smile to myself. I know I intimidate her. Hell, I've worked hard to be the person I am, and it's difficult to step outside the role I created for myself.

Placing my hands on her shoulders, I say gruffly, "Let me touch you, make you relax."

I start to massage her shoulders and feel the tension in them. As I press harder, she groans a little and my cock shifts, impatient to get on with this.

"So, think about what you like, darlin'. Think about my hands on your body and how good that makes you feel. Relax into it and picture the thing that turns you on the most."

I continue to press, to knead, to touch, and I just fucking hope she's not picturing that bastard from the bar right now as she moans softly and I feel some of the tension leave her.

"Does that feel good, darlin'?

"Yes, sir."

I'm almost blinded by lust as I touch the soft smooth skin of probably the most desirable woman to ever kneel at my feet.

It's almost too much and my cock throbs so hard it's uncomfortable.

"Turn around and face me."

She shifts and as she kneels at my feet, I feel a massive sense of control, a power that hits me like an instant fix. Her beautiful blue eyes look up at me and she chews on her lip, I watch a faint blush creep across her cheeks as her breathing intensifies. Skye is probably the most beautiful woman I've ever seen and she steals the air from my lungs and makes time stand still.

Rubbing my thumb across her lips, I watch her eyes heavy with desire and I whisper, "Have you ever seen a man naked before?"

She nods and a small smile tugs on her lips.

"In movies mainly, but then again, I do have a brother who isn't careful about covering up."

She laughs softly and I stare at her in amazement. "How have you stayed so innocent? Was there no past boyfriend, anyone at all who tried to take you before?"

I almost doubt her words because this doesn't seem right, but she shakes her head and a sadness enters her eyes. "I've made out countless times, but I never met anyone I wanted to know more intimately. When I met James, he was so different to the others. He was a man, and the rest were nothing in comparison to him."

"How long?"

"About five years." She laughs with embarrassment. "Shows you how sad I am. When I first set eyes on Professor Adams, I was mesmerized. He was good looking, well dressed, and had a commanding air about him that made me interested. The way he looked at me made me think I was special. I was at an impressionable age and it always felt as if we had this shared bond. Something forbidden and I would imagine all sorts of things, while I dreamed of us being together one day."

She looks down and I tilt her face to mine and say softly, "Don't be ashamed of your past, darlin'. You did nothing wrong; you just had a dream and there's nothing wrong with that."

"Thank you."

She smiles through bright eyes and I think on what she said. Five years is a long time to build up anticipation, and now I know why she was so shattered that night.

"So…" I smile somewhat wickedly. "Then you need to learn not to feel embarrassed around a man's body."

I reach down and lift my t-shirt off and love the interest in her eyes as she stares at my chest. I almost see her mouth drop open as I lean back and say with a hint of the devil inside me, "Unfasten my pants."

She looks worried as she nervously moves her fingers to my waist and starts to undo my jeans and I growl, "Look at me."

She holds my stare and I see the uncertainty and worry in hers that's like an aphrodisiac to me.

I shift so she can pull them down and help her a little as she pulls them off, before pushing them neatly to the side. "Now the rest."

She gulps a little and I can't believe I'm enjoying this as much as I am because watching her step outside her comfort zone is a major turn on.

Her chest heaves as she grips them and just feeling her soft hesitant fingers against my skin, almost makes me move this on a few steps as she appears to reason with herself and eases them gently down, my cock springing free and excited for what's coming. Her eyes widen and I see a small shiver as she contemplates what's before her and reaching down, I grasp my shaft in my hand and gently move it up and down, saying forcefully, "Look at me."

She blinks and looks up, and as our eyes connect, I feel a surge of protectiveness toward her. I need to make this experience one she will never forget for all the right reasons this time. She is trusting me not to hurt her, and so I smile gently. "Are you ok, darlin', not uncomfortable?"

"I'm ok, sir." Her breathing is fast and her words slow, and I smile to myself.

"Touch it."

Nervously, she reaches out and touches my cock, lightly as if she's almost afraid and I think it's my turn to hold my breath as I feel her soft fingers close around it.

"That feels so good, baby."

She smiles a little and I say gruffly, "Come and sit beside me."

She does what I say and I smile. "That wasn't so bad, was it?"

"No." She returns my smile and I place my arm around her shoulder and draw her head to mine and stroke her hair like a pet. "You see, darlin', you need to be comfortable with what you're doing, not be afraid, relax and want this more than anything. Don't ever let a man make you do something you're uncomfortable with because you won't enjoy the experience."

I sound like a hypocrite as I think on all the women who have been mighty uncomfortable as they anticipate my next move, but just thinking of Skye in that position seems so wrong. What the fuck is happening to me?

CHAPTER 11

SKYE

This is so different from what I imagined. He is so different and as I sit beside him exposed in every way, any nerves I had have been replaced with something else. Desire. Just feeling him stroke my hair, massage my shoulders and hearing his soft words wash over me, makes me relax into a situation that should have me tense and afraid. Slade is so different from the rumors I've heard. The brutal lover who loves to take a woman by force and reward her with pleasure. I've heard them talk and always wondered what makes a man so cruel but they must have been talking about somebody else because this man is different to that.

He continues to stroke my hair and the crackle of the flames in the fire is the only sound in the room as I adjust to a situation I never thought I'd find myself in. The most surprising thing of all is the ache between my legs. I am so wet down there for him. It's almost as much as my need for James, and that surprises me more than anything. I always thought I wanted James because of our deep connection. I have no connection with Slade, but my body seems to disagree.

It feels so good sitting beside him, skin on skin, looking into the flames and anticipating what comes next. After a while, he says softly, "Do you ever wish your life was different?"

"Yes."

He nods and carries on stroking my arm. "Tell me about your family."

I'm a little surprised by this conversation and say with a smile on my face, "They are the best. Mom and dad live across town and manage the other bar. Grady, my brother, has a tattoo shop." Shifting, I point to the dragon that curls up his arm and laugh softly. "I'm guessing you know that already."

He grins, "I may have met him occasionally."

"I can see that."

Unlike me, I get a bravery from somewhere and study the ink that covers every part of his arm and run my fingers over the intricate art that creates a masterpiece. "Well, when Buck died, Aunt Rose was left on her own to run the bar. They had set up a partnership with my parents and although she had staff, she needed someone more permanent. I used to help out when I could through college and when I left, it was a natural step to work alongside her and manage the bar."

"Are you ok with that?" His voice is slightly husky and rough around the edges, and I love how it sounds. "Yes, I never had the usual dreams of an occupation. I majored in English, probably because it set me in front of James most days. Sad really when I chose a subject because of my obsession with the teacher."

He continues to stroke my hair and I say with interest. "What about you, did you go to college?"

He stills a little and then says roughly, "No, I studied a different kind of subject. One that I'm not going talk about because you need to trust me, not fear me."

He laughs softly to take the bite from his words and says almost sadly. "You see, darlin', I'm not the good guy. I'm not the man you should find and certainly not the man you want in your bed. I'm a whole lot of fucked up and decent women like you should run screaming because I am the shadows in your nightmares and the man your mother warned you about, not to mention the man who's the reason your daddy can't sleep at night. You should be with someone worthier than me, so if you value your sanity, don't delve into a life that gave up living years ago."

His words make my soul weep as I sense the defeat in his voice. Whatever broke Slade Channing is breaking him all over again on repeat because he has given up on life before he has begun to live.

I say nothing and yet want to make it right for him, so I stroke his arm in much the same way as he is stroking my hair and love that he shivers under my touch.

"So, what happens now?"

I need to know because for some reason, I am keen to move on to the next step. I'm almost salivating at the thought as I anticipate the next part of this lesson and he says huskily, "The first stage is kissing. I'm guessing you've done that before."

"I'm not that innocent."

I laugh softly and he shifts around to face me and to my surprise, he stares deep into my eyes and grips my face in both hands and says, "Kissing is the most intimate part, believe it or not. It's usually the first step in connecting with someone and letting them in."

He moves closer and I feel the need throbbing inside me as he slowly presses his lips to mine and I part them and let him in. His tongue enters my mouth and twists with mine, slowly, deliberately and with a firmness that commands. Our lips press against each other as he holds me in place and explores my mouth, tasting, touching and owning and this first contact is something I can deal with but it isn't enough. It's already not enough, and I groan against his mouth as I feel a desperate need for more. I feel the warmth of the fire heating my skin, but that's nothing to the inferno raging inside. My eyes are closed and this time I don't see James, I see Slade Channing. I feel him and want him so badly, I can't hold out much longer.

His hand moves to the back of my head and pulls me in deeper, and as I feel his rough stubble grazing my face, it sends me wild. My body appears to have a life of its own as it shifts closer, craving his against it; wanting more; wanting him.

My heart is beating faster and I wonder if it's strong enough to last because this is stage one, a kiss for Christ's sake. What will I feel when this becomes more intimate?

Suddenly, he pulls back and my breath is fast as he pushes the hair from my face and whispers, "You feeling comfortable, honey?"

"Yes." My voice has an edge to it that makes him smile and he laughs softly, "I'm in a strange situation here because I'm taking things slow. I just want you to know, I don't do this. I don't kiss a woman and I don't hold back."

I stare at him with a sudden burst of emotion for the man who is surprising me every second that passes. "You don't."

He shakes his head and smiles sadly. "Not really my style, darlin'. Anyway, maybe it's time we grabbed some food; you must be starving."

I feel so disappointed because I really thought we were going to do this right now, and he laughs, "One step at a time and by the time I get to the most intimate part of our lesson, you will want it more than you have ever wanted anything, even that fucking bastard you fell in love with."

At the mention of James, my face must fall and Slade says

a little angrily, "He didn't deserve what you gave him and you didn't deserve what he did. I want to show you how it should have been, so you never settle for less. You are a beautiful, strong woman, who is weak due to inexperience. That is why I agreed because the thought of you repeating that mistake with the next guy, wouldn't sit well with me."

He stands abruptly, not realizing his words have crushed my soul. The next guy. Why can't I see past him? Why don't I want another guy and why have sudden feelings crept into this for a man I should despise? We have shared one kiss, that's all, and yet for some reason, the thought of him walking away from me so soon, is cutting me deeper than what happened with James.

CHAPTER 12

SLADE

I can feel Skye's disappointment, which makes the sadistic bastard in me laugh like a maniac. Denying us both the ultimate pleasure turns me on way more than it should. I want her more than she wants me, but I'm not rushing something that needs time. So, I head outside and fire up the barbeque because I wasn't kidding; we need to eat before anything else.

Luckily, the cabin is stocked with everything we need and as I wait for the heat to build; I think about this place. We've had this cabin my whole life and used to come here as kids. Sawyer and I grew up playing in this forest and mom and dad were always happier here. We have kept the inside exactly as she left it because mom loved the prettier things in life. She was always so beautiful, so elegant, and my dad adored her even more than we did.

I push away the memories because I can't let them destroy this moment because they would, as they have destroyed me. Living with what happened has made me the man I am today, which is why I can't let my feelings for Skye inside my heart. She will walk away after this because I will push her. I know she'll think she's a little in love with me. It's natural after what we will share. I *need* to make her fall in love with me to give her the experience she deserves. Not because I'm a kind, caring lover but because I want to make this right for her so she will never settle for anything less in the future.

Just thinking of Devon fucking Santiago touching her and using her as I'm sure he intends on doing, makes the rage burn deep inside me. That is driving this because I want to mark Skye inside this time, not outside because the thought of doing what I usually do to a woman, doesn't give me any desire to do it to her.

She's different, special and so she gets a different experience from the rest and the strangest part of all is that I'm loving every minute of this.

As I cook the sausages, I laugh to myself as I picture my next lesson. I wonder what she'll make of it and as she heads my way with the large robe tied around her waist, I can almost taste the anticipation in the air as she says huskily, "Where do you want these?"

She is carrying the bread and plates, and I nod toward the table. "Over there. There's some ketchup in the cupboard and beers in the fridge. Bring them outside, we'll eat out here."

She nods and heads inside and as I watch her go, something hits me hard. I like her here. I wasn't sure about bringing a woman to the cabin; I never have before, preferring the Castle instead. The Castle is what we call the clubhouse at the Dragon's Ruin, and usually I fuck my women there. There are no hearts and roses, no seduction, just taking something they are always willing to give and without care or thought to how they feel about things.

Usually, I fuck them in the bar with the other guys looking on, then I drag them upstairs and tie them to my bed. Sometimes the rage clouds my judgment and I take out my frustration on them first, inflicting pain before the ultimate desire.

My fingers close around the blade that is never far from my side as I think about how I cut them, loving the way it slices their perfect skin, the blood seeping through the crack like the devil's tears. I'm a sadist of the worst kind, and then I wash away their tears with the kind of loving I'm known for. Multiple orgasms and a night they never forget because I want to leave them with more than a physical reminder of my touch. I want to own their soul as well, and so I'm the biggest monster there is because I inflict pain and pleasure and love every fucking second of it.

As she heads back, she looks up and smiles and my heart shifts. She looks so different to my usual women. Unspoilt, beautiful, innocent. A princess that deserves a prince, not the bastard she's asked to do something no decent girl should ever think of, let alone say out loud. She trusts me and that has heaped a whole lot of responsibility on my shoulders I'm not used to and I'm struggling with that.

"Hey," She smiles shyly as she stands before me and hands me a beer. "I thought you could use this."

"Thanks."

My fingers close around the bottle and I feel a strong urge to touch her. To feel her skin on mine, hear her gentle moans of desire, see her smile at me as I drive inside her and love her like I've never done before. I think my whole life flashes before me right now and I take a step back. This isn't happening, I must close down and guard my heart because I know this is not going to have a repeat performance because when we head home, she is never going to want to see me again.

She looks around with interest and peers over my shoulder. "Hot dogs, how yummy."

She winks and I laugh softly. "You like."

"Who doesn't love them?"

"Then grab your plate and take a couple. You'll need to eat and will appreciate something hot inside you."

She giggles and turns and as she does her robe falls open a little, revealing her perfect breasts. Just seeing them earlier was enough to blind me. I knew they were impressive when I saw them straining against her t-shirt but seeing them loose and looking so amazing, has imprinted on my memory and I am desperate to know what they feel like in my hands.

She holds out her plate and looks at the sausage with greed and I flip a couple on her plate and say dismissively, "There, you may sit and eat."

She heads across to the table and as I join her, I place myself opposite just so I can watch her eat, because I chose this food for a reason, a perverted one and I'm already hard thinking about it.

She sits before me and doesn't disappoint, and as she places it in her mouth, I stare at her hard. Watching her tongue wrap around it almost makes me come on the spot and as she chews, she groans with appreciation. "This is sooo good."

A little piece of sauce sits at the corner of her mouth looking like blood, and I feel the heat tearing through me. I can't control the beast inside as I say sharply, "Take off the robe."

"What, here?"

Her eyes are wide as she looks around and I nod. "Here."

To her credit, she does as I ask and sits shivering a little in the open air. It's not cold, but there is a cool breeze and I watch her nipples harden as the cold air hits them.

"Eat." My tone is forceful with an edge to it I haven't used before and yet she appears to like it as her eyes dilate and she licks her lips, before slowly pushing the hot dog into her mouth. She holds my gaze and chews slowly, and there's silence as she sets a challenge in those eyes. I know she's turned on, wants me to do something we are both craving right now, but all I do is watch like a predator sizing up its next meal.

She finishes and makes to wipe her mouth and I say harshly, "Leave it."

Her hand drops and I say gruffly, "Get on the table."

"What do you mean?"

Her eyes are wide and I growl, "Lie with your back to the table."

She looks worried and I say softly, "It's ok, darlin', this is where things start to get interesting."

As she does what I say, I watch her with a hunger that's not for food and as she shifts into position, I stand and look down at her from the end of the table. Then, leaning down, I kiss her lips softly and lick the residue of food from her mouth, tasting meat and sauce and something so sweet, I could taste it all night.

Then I trail my kisses to her neck, biting and licking, kissing and sucking until she groans. My hands physically ache to touch her, but I hold the table edge and use my mouth instead, as I move lower and run my tongue around her nipple. She gasps and I deepen the kiss, sucking her breasts into my mouth and relish the groans as she arches toward me. I could feast on these tits all day, but I move lower and love the way she moans with pleasure when I reach the place I want to taste the most. I take a long deep sniff of the scent of a woman and as her legs part a little to welcome me in, I see the trail of honey that I want more than air and as I lick her front to back, she calls out, "Oh, god."

Laughing to myself, I am enjoying teasing this woman and take her throbbing clit in my mouth and suck it gently. "Oh god, Slade, that feels so good."

She shivers and as I suck, lick and taste her, I love every

second of it because I have never tasted honey as sweet as this.

Her orgasm comes fast and as she calls out, I relish the sweet sound as she comes so hard, she physically shakes and when I step back, I look down on a woman who is opening up to me like the rarest bloom.

Fuck me, she's impressive.

CHAPTER 13

SKYE

Slade Channing is a god. A sex god, because who knew I could feel so much pleasure from his tongue alone? I am shivering, not with cold but with desire—for him. Why him? His sort is not for girls like me. I never wanted a biker, unlike many of the girls who come into my bar. But there is something so deliciously dangerous about the scarred man who hardly says two words, yet is showing me something so beautiful I want more.

Lying on the wooden bench, naked and exposed to him, is the weirdest experience of my life. He is still fully dressed, yet I don't care. He is giving me the ultimate pleasure and as I feel his soft tongue touching a place I have let no man before; I shiver with desire and want more—oh, so much more. I want him. Not James, definitely not James, because this experience couldn't be more different to the one the other evening.

Slade continues kissing, sucking and driving me insane and my heart races so fast I almost can't keep up. The pressure builds so much it shatters and brings with it a wave a pleasure, the like of which I have never experienced before.

I'm almost embarrassed as I scream, "Oh God," and feel my pussy throbbing so hard I wonder if it's having a seizure.

Slade just stands at the foot of the table and watches me as if I'm a prize exhibit at the zoo and it should feel uncomfortable, but it doesn't. It's so wrong; I know that, but I don't care because I want the whole experience and he is certainly not holding back.

To my surprise, he scoops me up in his arms and as I bury my face in his hard chest, he whispers, "You are so beautiful."

His words make me break a little inside because he sounds lost, wistful even, and I wonder if somewhere in the past his heart was broken. I don't like the thought of that because a surge of jealously shoots through me as I imagine him with someone else. That alone surprises me because if I'm sure of anything, it's that I'm one in a very long line of women who have been here before me.

He carries me inside to the pretty bedroom and lays me on the bed and as I look up at him, I feel the heat building once again as he rips off his t-shirt and I see a chest so beautifully decorate with ink, I take a moment to admire the work of art before me.

He grins with an arrogance that tells me he's used to admiration and then my eyes widen as he unbuckles his belt and slides it off, before turning his attention to his pants.

Slowly he unfastens them and I stare wide-eyed at a rock-hard cock that springs free and makes me full of desire and fear in equal measures. This is it; he's going to hurt me, I just know he is because surely that—well, that weapon, is going to tear me up inside.

For a moment, he stands naked before me and just caresses it, stroking it almost lazily as if he's in no hurry with this and all I can do is watch with a fear that's growing by the second. I'm not sure I'm ready to experience the pain I know is coming and then he says firmly, "On your knees."

I kneel before him on the bed and he says huskily, "Remember the hot dog?"

I'm suddenly aware of where this is going, and he says gently, "Take this in your mouth and get used to how it feels."

I nod, but I can't look at him because this is the most embarrassing moment of my life, even after lying naked on a wooden table being eaten by a hungry animal in broad daylight. This, though, is so intimate, so dirty and so wrong.

He grips my head with two hands and guides my mouth to his cock and as he pushes inside, I feel it's soft and smooth and not as unpleasant as I thought. Then he whispers, "Feel it slide to the back of your throat. Watch how your mouth accommodates it and hear how much I love it."

I close my eyes and do as he says and as he moves slowly and gently, I love hearing his muffled groans as he fucks my mouth. Tentatively, I suck a little and his sharp intake of breath gives me a confidence to increase the pressure. His fingers grip my head and this time I moan softly as I feel so turned on hearing how much pleasure I'm giving him. I'm not sure why I'm enjoying this so much. Just seeing him naked was an experience I'm unlikely to forget any time soon, but feeling him inside my mouth, filling it and owning it, is sending a wet trail to my pussy that is desperate to feel the same pleasure.

His pace increases and his fingers tangle my hair and he rides my mouth, groaning loudly and yet just when I think he's going to come in my mouth, he pulls out and only his heavy breathing betrays how turned on he is.

He places his finger under my chin and lifts my face to look at him, and I almost close my eyes because the intensity on his should be scaring me right now.

He looks magnificent as his eyes glitter and his twisted smile tells me I'm probably not safe as he says huskily, "See how good you make me feel. See how natural this is and feel the desire lighting a trail inside. Sex should be beautiful, a meeting of minds and bodies and only when you crave someone so much it hurts, should you let them in. When they make you feel beautiful, desired and as if you can't exist for another minute without feeling them inside, you should you let them in. Do you want me, Skye, do you desire what I can give you because you only have to say the word and I'll show you the ultimate pleasure?"

I nod and he growls, "I didn't hear you."

"Yes, I want to know what that feels like."

"Wrong answer."

He pulls back and steps away, and I feel a sense of panic I wasn't expecting.

"But…"

He stares down at me and growls, "You didn't say, sir, and you didn't say you wanted *me*. You see, you need to want me, to crave me, to do everything in your power to make it happen, but you just want the experience and it could be anyone standing here. Sex is a meeting of souls and until you desire me and not the experience, we will do things differently."

He holds out his hand and smiles, which takes my breath away because Slade Channing never smiles. He is so serious, brooding even, and seeing how his face transforms makes my heart beat even faster, if that's possible. Slade Channing is absolutely the most beautiful man I have ever met and if I was disappointed before, now I'm devastated that he isn't inside me.

As his fingers close around mine, he says softly, "We need to talk."

CHAPTER 14

SLADE

This woman is driving me insane. Just my cock inside her mouth was enough to send me delirious. She is so innocent, which I'm discovering is the sweetest pleasure. Watching her learn something new is giving me a different kind of pleasure and I want more. I want the whole of her and I'm a greedy bastard because I don't just want her body; I want Skye Slater to fall madly in love with me and be ruined for any other man. Then I will walk away because I don't deserve a woman like her. Someone so beautiful, God almost gave up because he had created perfection and there was no other challenge. This is a different kind of sadism because breaking Skye's heart is something I never saw coming. I want to own this woman because the thought of her giving her heart to any other man is making my own physically break apart.

I take Skye's hand and lead her into the bathroom and run the water and add some oils that have been left here.

As the steam fills the small room, I turn and look at a woman so beautiful, it momentarily blinds me.

"I'm sorry, Slade."

She seems upset and chews on her bottom lip. Her eyes are filled with hurt and I can't look away as a powerful emotion sweeps through me.

"Why?" I'm interested to know and she says sadly, "I'm not sure I'm doing this right. I've disappointed you and you probably wish you'd never agreed to this."

I almost laugh out loud and just shake my head, maintaining a blank expression.

"How can you expect to know the game until you played it? I'm teaching you more than just physical things here; sex is more about emotions and feelings than anything else. You will understand that soon enough, so come, take my hand and I'll show you what I mean."

She holds out her hand and I entwine my fingers with hers and pull her hard against my body. Just feeling her tits graze my chest makes me instantly hard and as she feels my length against her, her eyes widen and she shivers a little. I dip my head and lightly nip her neck with my teeth and whisper, "Feel how much I want you, beautiful lady. See what you do to me."

I take her hand and guide it to my cock and take a moment to enjoy the sweetest pleasure. She moans a little and I know that she is throbbing with need and I smile against her skin.

"Do you like that my little one? Do you like feeling how much I want you?"

She whispers, "Yes, sir."

With a low moan, I capture her lips and taste them, biting, licking and sucking those lips, that when I saw them wrapped around my cock almost sent me feral.

She gasps as I plunder her mouth and pull her hard against me before running my fingers between her legs and caressing her clit. She cries out as I increase the pressure and slip one of them inside her heat and love how wet she is. She almost comes as I pump two fingers inside her and kiss her harder, with more passion, and she cries out, "Please..."

"What, darlin', what do you want?"

"I want you to show me how good it can be."

I smile against her mouth because she is such a good girl she can't beg me to do something she is craving right now, and once again I relish the power I have over her and pull back.

"Get in the tub, I'll join you soon."

Her face is flushed and not just from the steam, and her pupils are dilated and desperate for more of what I'm giving her.

As she lowers herself into the tub, I light the candles around the room before stepping in myself and settling behind her. Then I pull her body into mine and my legs fall either side of her and her head rests back on my chest.

"Do you like this, Skye?"

"Yes, sir."

Grabbing the soap, I start to wash her body, carefully, gently and she groans, "I love this."

Her soft voice turns me on almost as much as her body, and I'm loving how different she makes me feel. I'm not used to gentle persuasion. I demand, but that would scare the shit out of this girl, so I'm holding back and discovering a different kind of pleasure.

"I wasn't expecting it to be like this."

"Like what, darlin'?"

I carry on soaping her body and she laughs softly. "I never thought it would feel like this. I suppose I heard the rumors and thought you'd be more brutal, not so gentle and probably inside me by now."

"You were right then."

"About what?"

"I'm brutal, I'm cold and I don't feel, but we're not here

for me. This is about you, Skye. Your pleasure and what you want. I'm just showing you how good it can be."

"You mean, you're not enjoying this."

Her voice sounds hurt and I stop soaping her body for a moment and feel something tear through me that feels a little like regret.

"Darlin', I'm not Prince Charming. I'm not the good guy and I'm not the man your mama wants in your life. You asked a monster to show you something that should grow over time. Yes, it would be easy to throw you down, tie you to my bed and do the usual things my women experience, but not you. You're not ready for that and I doubt you ever will be."

She half turns and as she looks directly into my eyes, I see a flash of the steel that I saw before. The woman who takes no shit and knows what she wants.

"Why not?" She's angry and her eyes flash, temporarily blinding me. "Are you saying I'm not worth your time; I don't get to experience the real Slade Channing because I wouldn't cope with it?"

It would be so easy to show rather than tell at this moment but I don't want to witness the pain in her eyes that I saw that night, so I shake my head and sigh heavily, "Darlin', one thing's certain, we always want what we can't have and you know I'm right. You wanted your professor because it was forbidden. You built up longing for him over many years and told yourself he was your destiny. You saved yourself for him, and when that moment came, it destroyed you. I'm just saving you the build-up because honey, I would destroy you and it would be way more brutal than what he did to you, so just relax and know that you're the only woman I have ever treated the way I'm treating you."

I run my fingers through her hair and say gently, "I'm not

the man for you; you deserve so much more and never settle for less than that."

Leaning forward, I capture her lips in mine and show her rather than tell. I light the flame inside a woman who burns so magnificently, and she doesn't even know it. Skye is a rare creature indeed because she makes me see what I could have had if I hadn't fallen so far. I'm not going to see Skye again, or take her into my world because she will break. Like my mom, my beautiful, amazing, sweet, gorgeous, mom. Skye will be destroyed and I won't be the man responsible for that.

CHAPTER 15

SKYE

I'm drowning and not in the water that laps against my skin. I'm drowning in the many layers of Slade Channing. As I gradually peel them away, he reveals a more interesting, more desirable part of him that traps my heart piece by piece.

I want to experience the whole of him because I'm feeling a desperate need to crawl inside his heart and live there. He is a mystery to me and I can't work him out.

Pulling back, I stare into his eyes and my attention is drawn to the scar above the right one. It's jagged and looks painful, as if it was just left to heal without care. Running my fingers over the cut, I whisper, "How did you get this scar?"

He stills and I wonder if I've brought a bad memory to the surface and for a moment, I think he won't answer. Then he shrugs and says a little sadly, "I did it myself."

"What?"

I stare at him in total shock and he nods. "Has that shocked you; do you see now how many levels of fucked up I am? This scar represents that, darlin' and is a visual reminder of the sadist I am."

"But why?"

I trace it with my fingers and he shivers a little.

"It was after my mom died. I couldn't deal with the pain. She left me, she chose to inject a lethal drug into her veins and she left. She was so beautiful, so perfect; a lot like you. This cabin, this place, all these things, were her doing. We all loved her, so much it could be a little stifling at times. She was like a butterfly caught in a dirty trap because women like mom, like you, should never be married to bikers and the dirty lives they live. Turns out she hated the life, hated what she became and hated us because why else would she choose to die? So, in answer to your question, I cut myself, so that every time I look in the mirror, I see her. I see the ugly side to beauty because it reminds me not to expect more. I cut women because they are as lost as I am. They come to our club for only one reason, a good hard fuck and a biker to wear as protection. They want the pain; they want the rough love and they are desperate to belong. Have I shocked you, little Skye? Do you see how much of a devil sits before you? Do you want to lie tied to my bed while I take a blade to your perfect skin and mark you like I marked me and remind you how brutal life is? Because I won't, even if you beg me because you are the one thing in my life I can do right. I want you to want more. To find a man who will love you with all his heart. Someone who will protect you, care for you so deeply you feel the burn and someone who will never drag you down to the gutter to live like filth. You deserve everything and I can give you nothing, so push away any desire you may have to experience the whole of me because you would never survive."

He has such a wild look in his eye as he grasps my head and pulls me close, hard and roughly. He bruises my lips as he unleashes a passion that should terrify me but only makes me want more. He bites my lip until I taste blood and grips my chin hard so it bruises. He becomes a wild animal as he takes my hand and drags me from the tub, spilling the water over the edge in his haste.

Then he drags me to the bedroom and tosses me on the bed before facing me with his eyes blazing, and I stare at him in amazement. He is magnificent; even now, when he is doing his best to scare me away. I can't stop staring because now I know what all the fuss is about. This man feels so deeply he can't deal with what it's doing to him inside.

He breathes out slowly and I see him regain control and his eyes flash as he snarls, "Don't ask for something I'm not prepared to give."

"Where?"

My voice is soft and husky and he looks confused. "What do you mean?"

I shift up on my knees and sit before him. "Where do you cut your women, I want to know?"

He closes his eyes and exhales sharply. "We're not talking about this."

Grabbing his hand, I place it on my breast and whisper, "Is it here?"

Then I move it to my stomach, "Here?"

I take it lower until his hand brushes against my pussy, "Here; where do you mark them, I want to know?"

He turns and I swallow hard as he draws something from his jacket that is lying on the side. I see the steel blade flash as he says darkly, "Lie back."

I feel myself shaking inside as I wonder what the hell I've just done, and he runs the blade against my breasts, lowering it to my stomach and then it hovers against my pussy.

"Do you want to feel pain, Skye?"

His voice is rough and almost cuts me on the jagged edges. "Do you want to feel the blade slice your skin and spill your blood? Would it turn you on to know I'm responsible for scarring your beauty; a constant reminder of the devil you let into your bed in one foolish moment of need? A reminder for life about the damage humans do to one another inside and out and the moment when you sold your soul to the devil and let him control your mind."

The blade hovers over the skin of my right thigh and as I feel its blade teasing my skin, he says huskily, "This is where I mark my women, it shows the next man that they trusted another enough to let him do what the hell he wanted and loved every fucking minute of it. Do you want the mark on your body as a constant reminder of that because be careful what you wish for, honey, it's a dark road to travel?"

His breath is hot against my neck as he whispers dark words in my ear and I am so turned on right now, I would agree to anything. To feel some sort of release; to bleed out the pressure that is building inside and he growls, "First I tie them up, hands and feet so they are spread out before me. They can't move and I control every part of them. Then I cause them pain, a slap, a pinch, a scratch or a bite. I watch their skin change color and the angry bruises make me feel like a fucking king and you know what…"

"What?" My voice shakes and he grins like a madman, "They beg for more. So, I take my blade and watch it burn a trail against their skin. The blood seeps through the crack and they scream. They are conflicted and hovering between Heaven and Hell, and that is the moment I love the most. I love seeing them willing to do anything to please me, and that is what drives the animal you want inside you. That is why I will never give you that part of me because you, Skye, you are not like them, you are perfect and who would want to ruin that?"

He drops the blade and looks deep into my eyes and I lift my hand and stroke his scar and whisper, "You are wrong."

"About what?"

"This." I brush my lips against it and whisper, "This is the most beautiful part about you, Slade Channing. It reveals your soul. It shows how deeply you love and how much pain you surround yourself in. It shows me a man who is worth the fight, someone who could love so hard any woman would be lucky to experience that and if you think you're a monster, then who fucking cares because even a monster deserves love and you are denying yourself something that you deserve more than most."

He says nothing and just stares into my eyes and I smile shyly. "So, Slade Channing, sir. I'm begging you, put a girl out of her misery and fuck me so hard I will never forget you."

For a moment I think I've lost him as he closes his eyes and looks as if he's hurting inside. Maybe I've pushed him over the edge and he will lose control. I should be scared shitless right now, but I'm not. I'm balancing on the edge of something breath-taking and I want to fly.

Then his eyes open and the passion in them causes me to hold my breath, as he rests his head to mine and whispers, "Be careful what you wish for."

Then he lights a trail to my throbbing pussy as he kisses every part of my body with soft light kisses that burn. He creates a river of pleasure running through my body as he worships every part of me and as he laps at my arousal, I push myself closer, needing more.

I watch as he grabs a condom off the table and grins. "You sure you want this, honey?"

"Yes."

He raises his eye and I say quickly, "Sir, yes sir, I want this, I want you, I want Slade Channing."

He grins like the cocky bastard he is and I feel him hard against my opening and I bite my lip, this is going to hurt so badly.

He kisses me softly on the lips and whispers, "I'll take it slow."

As I feel him edge inside, I'm amazed at how my body welcomes him in. It parts naturally, and as his cock enters me, it feels like a delicious form of torture. It's uncomfortable and burns but not in the same way as before. I feel a sense of being filled completely, and any pain is soon replaced by the ultimate pleasure. I gasp as his groans make me even wetter, guiding him in and giving him a reason to stay. My heart beats frantically against his as I feel him inside and he moves his hand and flicks my clit, making me cry out.

"Oh, god."

He laughs softly, "Does that feel good, darlin'?"

"Yes." I arch my back and love how he fits even deeper inside, and as he gently starts to rock inside me, I feel an explosion of feelings deep inside.

He growls against me, "So fucking tight, so fucking perfect. You are everything I hoped for."

I can't speak because he fills every part of me with him and I want more. He increases the pressure and starts pumping harder, deeper and all the time he massages my clit until I can't take it anymore and a feeling of such intense pleasure rushes through my body like a river that's burst its bank and I scream out as I ride a wave, I never thought possible. He grunts and then roars his own pleasure as he joins me in ecstasy, and as we both reach a climax, that's been building for some time, the only thing I want is more.

CHAPTER 16

SLADE

What the fuck just happened? One minute I was in that dark place I retreat to when provoked. I could have cut Skye and she would have begged me for it. Then something shifted, and she trapped my soul. I entered paradise and I never want to leave. There was no fear, no pain and nothing but complete and utter love that filled my heart when I was inside her. She accepted me, the whole of me, and that means more than she will ever know.

Nobody sees this side of me, they want the danger, the excitement, and the bad boy. She wanted me, my past and every rotten part of me, and she let me in and filled me with love. Now I know I'm fucked because I want more of the same, and yet I know I can't. I must be true to my word and let her go, so she finds love with someone she deserves, not think she wants. But we're still here, so I have this time at least, and I'm in no hurry to leave, so I roll her on to her side and stare deep into her lovely eyes. "That's what love is, honey, that's what you should feel when you have sex."

Her smile is so bright it blinds me as she faces me with tears in her eyes. "Thank you."

Leaning in, she kisses my lips lightly, like a fairy dancing on the breeze and says softly, "I may just need you to run over that lesson again, sir. I mean, I would hate to forget it."

Laughing, I pull out and toss the condom in the wastebasket by the bed and reach for another. "If you insist."

I love the way her eyes widen in shock and I laugh. "Relax darlin', you need to recover from this lesson first. Come here."

Wrapping my arm around her, I pull her down onto my chest and stroke her arm lightly and love the way she snuggles against me with a satisfied sigh.

"What are you thinking?"

The words leave my lips and surprise me because I'm not known to care what women think.

She sighs. "This is nice; way more than I expected. I'm glad I asked now, although I couldn't believe the words actually made it out of my mouth. How embarrassing."

She giggles and I laugh softly. "It takes a lot to shock me, darlin', but you managed to do that in one sentence but for the record..."

I kiss her head lightly, "I'm glad you asked too."

"So, what happens next?" Her voice is hesitant and I smile inside. "We sleep and then if you want to go over anything, I suppose I can spare the time."

She looks up in shock and I wink and love how she instantly relaxes and smiles sweetly. "I think I do need to go back over it, all of it, actually."

Her eyes sparkle and my breath hitches at a sight that's unusual for me. I don't fuck innocent women. The women I take to bed are broken; much like me. They're hard, calculating and desperate; not soft, vulnerable and so beautiful they make my head spin. Skye is different, and that makes me different around her. Lighter, less trapped by my own demons. She makes my heart beat faster and gives me hope for something better.

She lays her head on my chest and says sleepily, "You *have* marked me, Slade Channing, you just can't see where."

I don't answer her and as her breathing relaxes and as she falls asleep, I stare at the ceiling, not moving a muscle. I can't sleep through this moment. I want to hear every sound, every moan, and every breath of a woman I will walk away from, for her own good.

She sleeps for close on two hours and I stay awake, loving every second. Her skin feels soft against mine, her breath fans my chest and her small moans as she sleeps, make me smile and long for her to wake, so we can repeat the performance. Just thinking of my usual behavior sickens me with her. I couldn't do it; I could never hurt this woman. I know I'm fucked because of my mom. I don't need a shrink to tell me that. The fact I loved her so hard and see it as a personal betrayal that she left is probably the reason I punish the women in my bed. They always leave and if they don't go willingly, I push them out. I can't ever feel again, it hurts too bad. It's why I prefer it this way. It allows me to survive.

Now there's Skye and this pocket of time we have made for each other. No one else knows, only us, and it's a delicious secret that will always be just that. A dirty secret for our knowledge only, and if Skye thinks it's anything more than that, she's in for a shock.

She stirs and looks up at me shyly. "I'm sorry, Slade, did I sleep for long?"

She looks embarrassed as she wipes her mouth and I laugh. "You do know you snore."

"I don't." Her eyes are wide with horror and I nod. "Terribly, it's why I couldn't sleep, you know."

"You're lying."

"You think, how do you know? I mean, this is the first time you've slept with a man, unless you've been lying to me."

Her face flushes and she looks mortified, which makes me laugh out loud. "Relax, darlin', I'm messing with you. Now, why don't we grab some clothes and I'll show you around."

"Really." Her eyes light up and I nod, feeling generous for once. "It's a beautiful place; it's a shame not to see that."

We make short work of dragging on our clothes and seeing her dressed in jeans and a tight tee, makes me hard all over again. Skye Slater could so easily become my woman. It would be easy to persuade her to stay. I know the signs, the little looks, and wistful stares. The fact I've been so gentle with her and made her experience a completely different one to what I'm usually known to provide—but I can't. It's not fair - on her.

Pushing away the disappointment that brings me, I grab her hand and love how it feels in mine.

"Come on, we need to work up an appetite."

CHAPTER 17

SKYE

I am falling in love with Slade Channing. This wasn't supposed to happen. I was meant to learn what makes sex good and walk away. I'm meant to find a decent guy, one who won't hurt me, or make me feel cheap. Slade would probably do both those things, but I don't care.

I like him. His company, his conversation, the look of him and his wit. I like the way he makes me feel special and gets me to agree to anything he wants to give because I know he won't hurt me. Even when he ran the blade against my skin, I trusted him. He could have cut me and I would have accepted it. I *want* to be marked by this man, have a permanent reminder of him. I totally understand his reasons for cutting his face, it's a reminder of his mom every time he looks in the mirror. Well, I want a reminder of him, of this time, and I wonder if he'll agree to it.

We walk through the trees and I gasp with pure pleasure.

"This view is breath-taking."

"It sure is." He catches my eye and the look he throws me melts my heart. Somehow, we take a step closer and as he dips to taste my lips, I run my hand around the back of his head and pull him closer.

Kissing Slade is the ultimate pleasure because it's like a window to his soul. He lets me in and I'm grateful for that because he makes me feel special, different to the other girls, and I wonder why he's never met anyone.

"Why are you alone, Slade?" I whisper the question and he stiffens.

"I like it that way."

He pulls away and stares broodingly over the mountain and I can tell he's unhappy I asked. Changing the subject, I sigh and say sadly, "Do you think I'll ever meet someone; ever meet a man who treats me well?"

"Of course, you deserve nothing less."

"But what if that respectable man turns out to be like James—a wolf in sheep's clothing? It could happen."

"It could, I suppose that's why you should hang back a little, test them out before you commit, or do anything you'll be ashamed of."

"Like this." He turns sharply and I shrug.

"It's not really something I can talk about—I mean, how would that make me look? You - it will just reinforce the legend; me - I'll look like a whore."

"Then don't tell."

He looks away and I know he's pulling away from me. He doesn't want to forge any kind of connection with me outside of our agreement, and that hurts like hell.

I look around at the beautiful scenery and feel so lucky to be here at all. The memory will keep me warm at night while I wait for something magical to happen and all my dreams to come true.

Slade's voice punctures my thoughts as he says sharply, "Skye, stop thinking."

"You can't tell me to stop thinking—asshole."

I grin and he rolls his eyes. "I mean it. Stay focused and stop dreaming. When you return, you will know what happens when a man takes a woman and she loves every minute of it. I'm guessing you feel different to last time because you wanted this."

"I wanted him." My shoulders sag a little and he says sharply, "And now?"

"I hate him." I whisper the words and wrap my arms around me and shiver. "I was saving myself for him and I thought it would be amazing. I thought he would ask me to be his girlfriend and I suppose that's why I got carried away."

"He will come back."

Slade's voice is curt and I shrug. "Maybe, but I'm not sure if I want to see him again. Perhaps I should take Devon up on his offer and try it with him. I've got to start somewhere and his may be the best offer out there."

Slade is by my side in a heartbeat and grabs me so forcefully, I feel a sudden fear. "Do not, under any circumstances, go anywhere near Devon Santiago."

"Why not?"

"Because he's a bastard and only wants one thing—you in his bed, against his wall and on the floor of his office."

"Takes one to know one, I suppose." I stare at him with anger and he nods. "Exactly. I know Devon and I know his world. Stay away."

"Fine, have it your way, but after this, you don't get to control my life. If I want to fuck Devon Santiago, I will and there's nothing you can do to stop me, unless…"

"It's your choice."

He cuts me off and says roughly, "We should head inside, there's a storm building."

Almost as soon as he says the words, the heavens open, and the rain comes down so hard it takes me by surprise. He grabs my hand and we run through the trees as the lightning cracks above our heads and the rain plasters against my face.

It was so sudden, so quick, without warning, and as we fall into the cabin and bolt the door, I look at Slade in shock.

"Wow."

He nods. "Happens a lot here. One minute it's brilliant sunshine, the next judgment day."

He rips his clothes off and leaves them in a wet heap and says shortly, "Strip, you can find your robe while I make us some coffee."

He doesn't even look in my direction and I have a sinking feeling this is the beginning of the end for us. He's pulling away and I hate every minute of it.

Quickly, I grab my robe and sit on the couch with my knees to my chest, loving the warm flames of the fire warming my shivering limbs.

Slade returns dressed in another robe and hands me a mug of steaming coffee and sits apart from me on the couch.

"Is everything ok?"

"No."

"What's wrong?"

He looks away like a petulant child and says shortly, "This–you–me–it's all wrong."

"Why?" I can hear the disappointment in his voice as he shrugs. "We should never have come and you should never have asked me."

"But…"

"Stop talking." He turns away and I sit slightly shaken as the man retreats into the dark place he normally lives. For a while we just sit watching the flames and then out of nowhere, I find a little bravery and shift across and take his hand in mine, leaning my head on his shoulder and press light kisses against his chest.

He stiffens and I say softly, "I'm sorry, Slade. You know, I would ask you again because I've loved every minute of this and just for the record, if you had cut me with that knife, I would have loved seeing a reminder every day for the rest of my life of this time here with you. A memory jogger, that's what it will be, and I suppose that's why you have your scar. A reminder of when you were happy and what you lost."

I shift around and drop the robe from my shoulders and stare deep into his eyes as I straddle his lap. Placing my hands on either side of his face, I drop my lips to his and take my time to kiss him like I've never kissed anyone before. I push his robe from his shoulders and moan softly as I feel his skin against mine and whisper, "Let me love you, Slade, just now, in this moment, let me show you how it feels to be loved."

I kiss his eyelids, his nose, and run my tongue inside his mouth. Reaching down, I stroke his hard cock that is throbbing with need. Rubbing my breasts against his chest, I gasp as I feel the pleasure this one simple act gives me and as I shift and lower my body onto his rock-hard cock, I try not to think about the last time I did this.

However, this time it's different. I *feel* different and it doesn't even occur to me that we're unprotected. That alone is the most foolish thing I've ever done because he could be riddled with sexual diseases. But I want to feel him, all of him, the man, unprotected and raw. As I gently rock back and forth, I gasp with pure pleasure as I feel him stroking me inside, touching parts of me I never knew existed and making me wetter than the mountainside after the rain.

A bolt of lightning lights up the cabin and the thunder that follows adds to the drama. I increase my pressure and yet Slade says nothing, just stares deep into my eyes the whole time and I can't read the dark look in his.

I can feel the pressure building, intensifying, and I want more. It's not enough and I run my hands over my breasts, pinching them to feel friction, anything to ease the pressure building inside.

Slade groans as I ride him and before I know what's happening, he lifts me up and I feel hot, liquid coat my abdomen. He roars my name and I stare in amazement as his seed coats my skin and he growls, "Fucking hell woman, that was close. You nearly got a permanent reminder of a different kind."

Then he starts to laugh and I can't help but join him as the lightning hits again and we lie glued together by his sex.

CHAPTER 18

SLADE

That was the most intense sex of my life. Skye took control and charge of a situation that shocked me into silence. I've created a monster because she was so perfect—in every way. Just feeling her wet pussy slide onto my shaft almost made me come the moment I was inside her. No fucking condom - what was she thinking? I can't remember *ever* doing it without one before and now I've had a taste of how good she feels, it's tempting not to go back.

Just seeing her riding my cock was enough to ruin me for any other woman, and nothing I do or say appears to put this woman off.

I'm guessing she'd even let me carve my name on her and love every minute and the thought of that excites me, showing what a twisted bastard I am.

But seeing how beautiful she is, naked and happy to bring me pleasure, hits me hard in a place many never reach. My heart.

Conscious I got there before her, I lift her up and lie her on the fur rug and position myself above her. Looking down into her trusting blue eyes, I lean down and kiss every inch of her perfect face softly.

Then I reach those breasts that were made for my pleasure and spend way too long enjoying every inch of them. I bite, tease and suck, until her hips rise to claim my cock and I move down to deny her what she wants the most. I kiss every part of this woman and lick and bite her hard, and she cries out as she feels the sting of pain. I love hearing her moan as she whispers, "Mark me Slade, I want to see it." I just shake my head and carry on driving her insane.

Then as she orgasms so hard on my tongue, I hold her firmly until she stops shaking and pulling her up, I face her sitting in front of the fire and say regretfully, "I think we're done."

"What?" Her eyes fill with disbelief and I say with a cool detachment that is hurting me way more than her, "Lesson done - over. I've taught you sex; we should go."

"But… why?" Her voice shakes and I shake my head as I shrug into my robe.

"I have things to do; you've taken up too much of my time already. Get dressed, the storm will be over soon and we'll head back."

I turn away so I can't see what being a bastard does to a woman like her and head to the shower because that took all my inner strength and has destroyed my heart. I must be cruel to be kind where it involves Skye because I could so easily make her mine forever, but she would be destroyed. Maybe not now, not next month or next year, but she would be destroyed, ruined and probably dead, if I was selfish enough to keep her.

Skye is angry. I can almost taste it as she waits fully dressed, clutching her bag.

Making sure to lock up the cabin, I take her bag and stow it on the bike before handing her the helmet, which she pulls down hard on her head and then turns away.

Feeling like the worst bastard in the world, I sit astride my bike and try to ignore her arms holding me tight as we head back to reality.

I think I change my mind about Skye fifty times over on the ride home because I know how upset she is, but it's probably nothing to how I'm feeling inside. I have to be strong enough for both of us, and I hate myself more than she probably does for what I just did.

By the time we reach the Dragon's Ruin, I know this will be the hardest part as she rips the helmet from her head and stares at me with tears streaking her face. The pain in her eyes is too much to bear as she says in a hollow voice, "I owe you for your time, name your price."

For a moment, I just stare and she returns it with an angry look and I shrug. "Just stay the hell away from me; that's all I ask."

She tries so hard to keep the tears inside, but I see them filling her eyes as she says roughly, "Fine by me."

As I hand her the bag, she snatches it out of my hand and walks away without a backward glance.

It's over.

I watch her car disappear and know I did the right thing. It hurts like crazy, but Skye needs me in her life like a fucking disease that will kill her in the end.

As I lock the bike, I feel so much regret for everything I agreed to because Skye doesn't know that she gave me something I badly needed and I'm struggling to deal with that. She listened, she understood, and she looked inside my soul, past the bastard and into my heart. She loved me, really loved me because I saw the emotion in her eyes when she fucked me bareback.

"Where the fuck have you been."

Marina's hard voice interrupts my thoughts and I look up and see her tapping her foot impatiently on the step.

"What's it to you?" I stare at her angrily and she obviously doesn't care, or she's stupid because she carries on.

"Who was that girl?"

"None of your business."

"Is she coming around here again, I should know."

"No, she's not, and why should I tell you even if she was? You're the hired help, darlin' and you do what the fuck I tell you, so cut out the angry accusations and fetch me a beer."

Marina looks as if she wants to carve her own name on my face right now, but thinks better of it and turns on her heels and heads inside. As I follow her, my heart sinks. Back to this fucked up life of shit after wallowing in paradise. Can things get any worse than this?

CHAPTER 19

SKYE

I cried all the way home. It was going so well. I felt something so real with Slade and he threw it all back in my face and made me feel like one of his cheap whores. Why? He didn't need to do that? I thought we had an understanding.

By the time I reach the Coyote Bar, my head is back in business and as I make my way inside, I hope Rose doesn't ask me any awkward questions.

Luckily for me, Grady is working and knowing my big brother, he wouldn't blink if I came in naked with stab wounds all over my body.

"Hey sis, good break?"

"Fine, thanks." My voice is unnaturally high, and he nods. "Good. Bars been busy until now; I'm looking forward to getting back to the shop."

"Where's aunt Rose?"

"Sleeping it off in the back."

He looks up and sighs. "It's not good all the whiskey she drinks. Someone needs to enroll her in a program or something."

"She's grieving."

"It's been four months already and she'll be dead if she carries on this way. You need to get her to see someone."

"Why me, what about you, or mom?"

"Because you're close to her, that's why?"

"I'm ok." Rose heads into the bar and fixes Grady with a sharp look. "I can hold my drink and I can take it or leave it. Just because I choose to get wasted, it's no business of yours."

She turns to me and smiles. "Good trip?"

Unlike Grady, she stares at me sharply and I wilt under her gaze. "Yes, lovely."

"Where did you say you went again?" Her tone is light, but her eyes are sharp and I turn away. "To the mountains with friends. Anyway, I should unpack and start bottling up. If it's as busy as Grady says, it will be a long night."

Quickly, I head to my room before she can ask me any awkward questions and as I strip and let the hot steam of the shower wash away every last trace of Slade, my tears join them as I cry as if I've also had a death in the family.

He was so kind and loving one minute and brutal the next. Something switched inside him and made him so cold it froze me out.

I'm not sure where I go from here because I fell in love in those mountains and now I've got a broken heart to heal for my troubles. I'm not sure if it was worse when James destroyed my hopes and dreams, or now, but either way, I am so done with men, period.

∽

I THROW myself into my work and Grady wasn't lying. The bar *is* busier than usual. Aunt Rose pitches in and I seriously think we need to hire extra staff because even though I have a team of five, it's nowhere near enough.

Once again, half way through the evening, I hear the customers talking and look worried and I know that Devon is outside. I'm not sure if I want to deal with another biker so soon after Slade, so I stay where I am. It's only when he heads inside, filling the space with menace, that I sigh and face him wearily. "What can I get you?"

I don't even pretend to be angry, just resigned to the fact he will keep on trying until he either gets bored, or I give in.

He smirks. "Did you miss me, darlin'?"

A shiver runs through me as I picture the last time someone called me that, and I try every trick in the book to push the memory of the man who said it away.

"No, I didn't."

I hand him a beer and as he tosses $20 on the counter, his hand closing over mine as I reach for it. Leaning in, he whispers, "Tonight, after you close up, we're going out."

"No, we're not." I snatch my hand away and he narrows his eyes. "Non-negotiable, darlin', it's time we moved this thing on."

"Excuse me, but do you have ears, because I just said no? Do you want me to spell out what that means because get it into your thick head, I'm not interested?"

His eyes flash and I make to turn away because I can't deal with him right now and he catches my arm and whispers, "If you don't, I will bring my club here every night. We will make this our regular and soon you won't have any customers left to serve. Your choice, honey, accept this is gonna happen, or risk losing your business. I treat my women right and expect something in return."

"But I'm not your woman."

I stare at him in horror and he winks. "You are baby, you just don't know it yet."

He takes a swig of the beer and turns and heads out of the door and I stare after him in shock. Surely, he doesn't really think that because if he does, my day has gone from extremely bad to catastrophic.

Aunt Rose heads over. "What did he want?"

"Me, apparently."

She looks worried. "That's not good."

"You're telling me, what am I going to do?"

"I'm not sure. Tell him no, don't encourage him, buy a gun. I really don't know the answer."

"You think I haven't told him I'm not interested already? The man's got no idea of the meaning of the word no. He's coming to collect me after we close tonight, do you think I should leave the State, go into hiding because surely if I'm not here he'll give up?"

"You could swap with your father, work the Coyote Bar across town."

"That won't work, it's the first place he'll look when he sees dad in my place. What am I going to do?"

"We'll think of something, don't worry."

I carry on working, but my head is all over the place. This is a disaster. Devon Santiago is the president of the Dark Lords for Christ's sake, even worse than the Dragons. Why on earth is he bothering with me when there must be a line of women stretching around the block of his club house?

Nothing I think of can put off the inevitable and by the time we close up for the night, I'm resigned to going on one date with the bastard and just hope I can do enough to put him off me for good.

CHAPTER 20

SLADE

As soon as I hit the desk, I got my head into business. I must have been at it for three hours when Marina pokes her head around the door, looking worried. "You've got visitors."

"Who is it?"

"You'd better come and see for yourself."

I make my way outside and my heart sinks when I see a group of Dark Lords littering my yard with their motorbikes and unwelcome expressions of anger.

Devon stares at me long and hard, and I see his sister Demi shivering behind him.

"What's up?" I nod and flick my cigarette to the ground, and Devon pulls his sister off the bike and removes her helmet.

She looks down, but not before I see the cuts and bruises on her face that look painful.

"Do you know anything about this, Slade?"

Devon's voice can only be described as controlled rage, and I shake my head. "No, what happened?"

Devon looks absolutely furious and says angrily, "Are you sure about that because word is you were missing last night and as it happens, my sister came back the very next morning looking like one of your usual victims. She won't tell me who attacked her, but I'm guessing I'm looking at him."

"You're not." I look at Demi and shake my head. "Tell him it wasn't me, darlin'."

She says nothing and looks to the ground and Devon hisses, "It looks as if you've touched my sister for the last time, Slade."

I see my own men step out behind me and to the side and can see this shit escalating fast if I don't do something about it, so I turn to Demi and say softly, "Who did this, darlin', tell us and we'll deal with it?"

She looks up and fixes me with a look I know only too well, and immediately I sense a trap. She says in a quivering voice, "I'm sorry, Slade."

Devon is so angry I fully expect him to pull a gun on me and he shoves his sister so hard, she falls at my feet. "Take her, she's your problem now."

"What the fuck…"

He nods. "You've messed with the wrong woman this time; you will make her your old lady and live to enjoy the benefits that bring. If you don't, you don't live, period. I'll have her stuff sent over."

He throws a disgusted look at his sister and before I can stop him, heads off in a haze of angry fumes.

Demi sobs in the dirt and I am so angry right now, I don't know what to do and just say in disbelief, "Why did you make him think it was me?"

As she looks up, I see the yearning in her eyes and know I've been trapped by a pro.

"I'm sorry, Slade, but you know Devon. He wouldn't believe me, anyway, this has your stamp all over it."

I am so angry I almost can't speak and yell, "Who was it?"

She shakes her head and I almost pull my gun out myself until Marina heads out of the clubhouse and shouts, "For fuck's sake, look at the poor girl, she's hurting bad. Come with me, honey, and I'll clean you up and then we'll get to the bottom of this."

She pushes past me and helps Demi to her feet, who half smiles as she walks past me, making the blood rush to my head. That's all I fucking need, a forced marriage with Devon freaking Santiago's sister, could my life get any worse?

I escape to my office for the entire afternoon and wallow in self-pity. When I woke up this morning, I had everything I wanted in life, now I have everything I don't want. How the fuck am I going to get out of this one?

A few hours later, Marina heads my way and shakes her head. "That was intense. What are you gonna do?"

"What did she say, did she tell you who did it?"

"She said it was you, was it?"

Marina looks unsure and I yell, "Of course it wasn't me, I was nowhere near the place, I was in the mountains."

"Yes, with her."

"What, don't be ridiculous, I was with that girl you saw on the back of my bike."

"I saw a girl, but it could have been Demi for all I know. Tell me, Slade, who was the girl and if it wasn't Demi, get her to back up your story."

Just thinking of what I said to Skye makes my heart sink. She won't say a thing because I told her not to and how would that look on her? She doesn't need to be associated with me, not her. I won't drag her into this mess and will find my own way out of it.

"I can't." I sigh and Marina looks at me sharply.

"Then we had better make the arrangements. Honey, it looks like you're about to gain an old lady, whether you like it or not."

CHAPTER 21

SKYE

During my entire shift, I'm stressing over what happens when we close. Not only that, but I can't shake my feelings for Slade, no matter how much I wish I could. He changed like a switch. One minute he was so loving, so into me—literally and then he withdrew in all aspects of the word. I get that he has issues. I think I would if I had his history and lived his life, but I was happy to work them through with him, but he was so cold and brutal and I feel as if he wrenched my heart out and stamped on it before tossing it off that mountain.

Grady left earlier and the staff are cleaning up. Aunt Rose retired hours ago and I'm left with a bad feeling about tonight. Devon Santiago is probably worse than Slade Channing. He has the bigger club, the darker reputation and an air about him that requires no argument. How the hell did I get into this and what am I going to do about it?

Maybe I could close up, turn out the lights and pretend no one's home. Even I know that wouldn't work; he would only turn up tomorrow with his whole club in tow.

With a sinking feeling, I know I must suck it up and go

out for one date. Hopefully, that will be enough to show him I'm not interested, not a sure thing, and not going to fall into bed with him.

Just thinking of what that would involve gives me the shivers. It was one thing with Slade; it felt right even though everything about it was wrong.

The door opens and I look up and see Devon darkening my doorway and the look he shoots me tells me I'm only doing one thing and that's heading out with him to god only knows where.

"Ready, baby?"

Sighing, I grab my keys and hope this is over quick.

He leads me over to his Harley and holds out a Dark Lord's jacket, which he wraps around me and pulls it tight. He leans in, still holding it and whispers, "I've been wanting to do this for a while now."

"What?"

I lick my lips nervously and before I can move, he fastens his lips to mine and pushes me back against the bike. I suppose I panic because this is too much too soon and I struggle a little and he steps back and laughs. "A fighter, I like that. I'm guessing you may enjoy it a lot more when you get to know me. Like I said, I treat my women well and you are the finest woman I know."

He wraps his arms around my waist and lifts me on to his bike before joining me and starting the engine. Handing me a helmet, he says darkly, "I ride fast, I hope you can deal with that."

Before I can object, he pulls out of the car park, kicking up the dust as we go.

Riding behind Devon is completely different to riding with Slade and it feels wrong to wrap my arms around his waist, but I need to if I want to survive. He wasn't kidding when he said he rode fast, and I'm wondering if circumstances will put me out of my misery before the date even gets started.

He drives to a part of town I don't go to much because it's not the sort of place young girls hang out. Trouble and poverty go hand in hand, and it appears that the Dark Lords like to inhabit the shadier side of town.

I look around me with fear because this place is scaring the hell out of me and I inch a little closer, and hang on tighter, as we power through the streets where dark figures linger in the shadows.

Devon stops outside a trailer and my heart rate increases as he cuts the engine and says gruffly, "Sorry, I need to make a quick stop and collect something before we head off. I won't be long."

"You're leaving me here." I stare around in fear and his grin is wicked and twisted. "You'll be safe here, darlin', they know this bike and if anyone touches you, they die. I won't be long."

He disappears before I can object and I try to make myself as small as possible because god knows who's watching me from the dark shadows surrounding us.

True to his word, he's soon back with a package that he stores on his bike. "Now, let me take you somewhere more in keeping with trying to impress a lady."

He grins and starts the engine, and the only place that would impress me right now is if he took me home.

No such luck and he takes me to an all-night bar on the edge of town and as we walk inside, he slings his arm around my shoulder and looks around him with authority. A waitress sashays up and pouts suggestively, "Devon, I was hoping you'd be here."

"Table for two, Patty, a private one."

She flicks her gaze over me and looks unimpressed, and Devon pulls me close and snarls, "Now would be good."

She nods and we follow her to a dimly lit booth in the corner of the room and she says petulantly, "You never call."

"And I never will, deal with it."

She leaves, looking as if she's going to murder us both, and Devon slides beside me into the booth and shakes his head. "As if I'd be interested in her. I have my sights set on a much classier woman, which is why I've been so patient."

His hand squeezes my knee making me almost jump out of my skin and luckily, another waitress comes and hands us some menus and fills our glasses with water.

Devon orders us a couple of beers and my heart sinks. He never even asked what I wanted. Typical alpha male, these guys have a lot to learn.

He leans back and groans, running his fingers through his hair. "Man, I've had a bad day."

"Same." I can sympathize with him on that score and he sighs heavily. "I had to deliver my sister to the Dragon's Ruin. Seems her loyalty lies there now."

At the mention of the Dragons my blood runs cold and I say in a high pitched voice, "Why, what happened?"

"Turns out she's gonna be his old lady and I can't say I'm happy about that."

"What, Slade?"

I'm surprised I can get the words out because the blood has rushed to my head and I'm struggling to breathe. Devon doesn't appear to notice and just grabs the beer the waitress delivers and takes a huge slug before ordering another.

"Shit happens, which made me think on us."

"Us, I didn't know there was an us." I'm still reeling after learning that Slade is about to get hitched and he turns and sets the beer down. My heart sinks as he runs his fingers around my head and pulls me close, his lips brushing against mine.

"It made me realize I need to settle down myself. Get my

shit together and make a life with a decent girl. There's no one I want more than you, so what do you say, honey, fancy being a biker's old lady?"

He doesn't even give me a chance to answer and crushes his lips to mine in a frenzied attack. All I can taste is beer and cigarettes, and I struggle to breathe. Somehow, his hands reach inside the jacket I'm still wearing and slip under my top, and I push him away.

"What the hell, don't you believe in taking things slow?"

He laughs and to his credit, leans back, once again reaching for his beer.

"Don't see the point."

"Well, I do. I'm sorry, Devon, but where I come from, people actually start dating. I know that may be hard to understand because I'm guessing you're used to women throwing themselves at you, but I'm not one of them and when you said you treated your women well, I believed you."

He has the grace to look ashamed and nods. "I'm sorry, you're right, I should have held back. The trouble is, baby, you're one hot chick and I'm having trouble keeping my hands off you at all."

I edge away as far as I can from him and grab my beer. "Well, I would appreciate it if you did. I'd like to get you know you first before, well, anything intimate."

He laughs but I fail to see the humor but that's not all that concerns me because out of the corner of my eye, I see something that makes me feel weak with pain. James is staring into a young woman's eyes a few tables along and as I stare in disbelief, he looks up and our eyes meet across the crowded room. He smiles and winks and I just stare in horror because I know the girl he is sitting with, she is a few years younger than me and definitely not legal and by the looks of it, they are not on a study period.

Devon follows my gaze and says in a deep voice, "Do you know that guy?"

"He was my teacher."

Devon laughs. "Looks as if he's taking his work home with him. Respect."

His words anger me. "What do you know about respect, that man's a monster?"

"In what way?" I now have Devon's attention and I whisper, "He stays single so he can date his students. Apparently, he waits until they leave college, but I'm not so sure in her case."

Devon shrugs. "Don't blame him, girls must throw themselves at him and it must be hard to ignore."

Once again, Devon annoys me and I'm grateful when the waitress comes to take our order. Devon the asshole, orders for us both and I can see what any future would be like with him. No thank you.

As I sit beside him, I feel trapped in more ways than one. But the main thing on my mind is the news about Slade. It hurts like hell to think he's dating someone and probably was before our mountain trip. The worst thing is, it's all my fault because he never promised me anything more than what I asked, but I thought we were more than that; it appears I was wrong.

CHAPTER 22

SLADE

I leave Marina to deal with Demi because I can't even look at the bitch. She has tricked her way into this club, and it's not going to be easy to send her packing. Just thinking on what she's told her brother makes me want to smash something, but I made it easy for her because I did sleep with her and she bears my mark. I will struggle to convince anyone it wasn't me and so I stay holed up in my office, dreading the moment when I have to deal with this shit.

Marina heads in around a couple of hours later with pizza and a beer and shakes her head. "You're in deep trouble, what are you going to do?"

"Beats me, Demi has it all worked out. Did she say anything, any clues who did this?"

Marina shakes her head. "She insists it was you and honey, it's not looking good."

I sigh heavily and lean back in my chair, and she looks at me with concern. "Give it a few days, maybe she'll slip up and then we've got her. Don't worry about it, there's business that needs attending to."

"What have you got?" It strikes me how different this is from when Axel ran this club and Marina was his old lady. Now he's off on a road trip and she's my right-hand woman. The first woman the Dragons have ever trusted with business and there is no one better for the job.

"That teacher you wanted checked out, it appears he's a bit of a predator."

My ears prick up at the mention of that freak and Marina shakes her head. "Word on the street is he likes them young. Not many speak out but a couple of the guys heard he likes to check into the Largo and never stays the night."

Thinking about the rotten motel on the edge of town makes my blood run cold. Rentals by the hour and the perfect place for men like the professor to lose themselves for a few hours.

"You got anyone on it?"

"Gibbs is keeping watch in case he checks in. I told him to snap some evidence and bring it to you."

"Thanks, darlin'."

I throw her a rare smile because Marina has been a nice surprise for me and in a different world, we were a couple for one night. How far we've come since then and I'm pleased about that because I've grown to think of Marina as family.

She smiles sadly. "I'm heading to the bar, you coming?"

"Why not?"

Deciding it's important to show my face once in a while, I go with her and when we push the door open, the loud music hits us and I see several of my men relaxing with beers and a willing woman on their lap. My heart sinks when I see Demi sitting in the corner looking out of place and her eyes light up when she sees me.

"Fuck this." I growl to Marina and she sighs.

"Suck it up for now, maybe you can have more luck with her. It wouldn't be the first time."

She sighs and heads off to find Damien, who appears to be her latest preference, leaving me to head over to our visitor.

"Hey." I grab the stool beside her and she smiles.

"Listen, Slade, I just want you to know I never meant to do this. It's just that when I rocked up this morning, Devon was waiting and jumped to the wrong conclusion."

"You could have put him right, why didn't you?"

She looks worried. "Because I didn't know who it was."

"What do you mean, were you attacked?"

She shakes her head and leans in closer. "You know me, Slade, we're two of a kind and I'm only telling you this because I feel as if I owe it to you."

"Go on." I light a cigarette and take a long drag, as she says huskily, "I've been going to parties run by the local mafia."

"Fuck, Demi, you know how to get yourself in shit. What happened?"

"I went to one last night, and it was a masked one. They provided the masks, and the place was crowded. You couldn't tell who anyone was, which was a good thing in my case because if Devon found out the company I was keeping, he would have gone in all guns blazing and started a war. Now, I may hate my brother most of the time, but I don't want his death on my hands, which is why I had to keep it a secret."

"So, what happened, did you play a bit rough?"

She smiles wickedly and I know that look. Demi and I share the same proclivities, which is why we got together a few times.

"It was wild, Slade. I had the night of my life and when Devon caught me sneaking in, I didn't correct him when he named you. What was I to do, I didn't think you'd mind covering for me?"

"Covering for you, I think the fact you've moved in and your brother wants us hitched, is pushing this a bit too far. To be honest, Demi, I really don't need this shit."

"I know." She looks down and sighs. "It's only for a few days, anyway, and we could have some fun while I'm here, I mean, why waste this opportunity?"

"No" I stare at her moodily and she laughs softly. "I've always loved you, honey, so gorgeous and dark, just how I like them."

"So, what's your big plan?"

"The guy I met is here on business and doesn't want any heat on him. I told him I'd lie low for a couple of days and then when he heads out of town, I'm going along for the ride."

"What man?"

She lowers her voice. "Some powerful suit who runs trafficking rings. He's so hot, honey, and seems quite into me. I'm heading off for a life of sin and if it doesn't work out, well, I'll just move on to the next club and meet someone else. This place is stifling me, and living with the Dark Lords is like living with animals. So, I'll be out of your hair in no time, no harm done."

She slides her hand on my knee and whispers, "One for the road, I'll make it a good one."

Just feeling her hand on me makes my skin crawl and my thoughts turn to Skye. She has ruined me for anyone else because the only thing that's been on my mind since she left is her. I wonder what she's doing now.

CHAPTER 23

SKYE

I am struggling on every level. Devon is seriously irritating me and he may be good looking, a guy most girls would love by their side but not me. I like my men less archaic and to have some form of conversation at least. His topic appears an interest in my tits and he can't appear to drag his eyes from them and I'm pretty glad of the jacket that I wrap around me like a shield. Then there's James, stealing glances and throwing me a look that tells me he's not done with me yet and there's Slade. I think my heart has broken just thinking of him with Devon's sister, probably in bed right now where I was a few hours ago. It's all too much and I have a headache coming on, so I endure another hour and then say weakly, "I'm sorry, Devon, this is all very nice and lovely but I really need to head home. I have to be up early and I have a raging headache."

"Sure, I'll settle the check."

If I'd have known it was this easy, I'd have spoken up half an hour ago and as we leave, I pointedly ignore my ex-teacher because now I see him for what he is, I couldn't dislike him any more if I tried.

The cool night air hits me and I take a few deep breaths because the atmosphere in the bar was stifling. Devon slings his arm around my shoulders, which I'm actually quite grateful for because it's a little cold out here.

We make it to his bike and he pulls me close and I resign myself to another lingering kiss because if I have to go through the motions, at least it will get this over quicker.

As his lips find mine, I let him in because I am destroyed and broken inside. Slade doesn't want me, he has someone else already and as for James, that is never going to happen. Devon is the last option and even though I want to curl up in a ball and sob my heart out, part of me likes this revenge kiss because I know that if Slade could see me now, he wouldn't like it one bit. It's that thought that drives me and as Devon's kiss deepens, I feel his hands grab my ass and pull me in and leave me under no illusions what he wants from me.

He whispers, "I want to be inside you so much it hurts."

I try to back off but his grip is firm and I laugh nervously. "I thought we were taking things slow."

"I am."

He kisses me again and I feel his hand inch up under my top and he grabs my breast hard and groans. "You turn me on so badly, come home with me."

"No."

I struggle against him and he whispers, "I'll make it good for you, baby, you won't be disappointed."

Luckily, a car heads our way and the headlights fall on us, making him pull away a little and I shove him hard and say tightly, "I just want to go home. As I said, I've had a bad day and need to *sleep*."

I emphasize the last word because if I went home with him there would definitely be no sleeping involved and I sigh heavily. "Please, Devon, I really do need to sleep."

It's all too much and my resistance is fading and to my

surprise he nods. "You've got it, but on the condition you'll see me tomorrow night. Maybe you'll be up for a night in instead, I'll order take out."

"I'm not sure, I need to visit my parents tomorrow, maybe another day."

For a moment I think he's going to blow because he looks at me with an impatience that tells me I'm not playing with a good guy here and then he nods and says roughly, "Fine, have it your way but baby, the next time we meet, you're coming home with me and I will show you just how good we will be."

I don't have the strength to argue and just accept my fate for now, but if I'm ever alone in the same room as him, hell will freeze over because I'd rather jump on a bus and head off with a one-way ticket to freedom.

∽

It's only when I'm in bed, alone with my thoughts, do I give into the pressure and cry like a baby. It's all too much. Today has destroyed me and the one thing I can't get out of my head is Slade in bed with his future wife.

∽

The next morning, even Rose looks concerned and I try to paste over the cracks and appear brighter than I feel but inside my heart is breaking. If I thought a night's sleep would help, it doesn't because my first thought when I woke was of Slade and what we were doing this time yesterday.

After going through the motions, by mid-morning Rose has had enough and hands me a coffee and says sternly, "Ok, spill the problem."

"What problem?"

She sighs. "I know that look, honey, hell, I've worn it often enough. It's a guy, isn't it? The teacher, or the biker?"

At the mention of a biker, my face must fall because she shakes her head and looks angry. "I knew it. They can't be trusted around good honest women. Now, this is what we're going to do."

I'm not sure what's she thinks but from her expression I'm not going to avoid it and she says tightly, "You need to get away, remove yourself from the situation and head across town to see your parents. I'll take over here and when that Dark Lord comes calling, I'll get rid of him—forever."

She looks concerned. "That is what you want, isn't it, honey?"

"I wish it was that easy." I stare into the mug gloomily. "Devon Santiago won't listen to you; I don't think he's even capable of understanding the most obvious signs. The man's got only one thing on his mind it seems and that's making me his."

Rose rolls her eyes. "They're all the same, macho pigs, the lot of them. No, you leave him to me and go and take some time out. You need to see your parents; it's been too long."

I can't even argue because the thought of getting out of here is an attractive one and I smile gratefully. "Thanks, I'd appreciate any help I can get. Will you be ok though, I mean, we are talking about the Dark Lords here?"

"Leave it with me, honey, I have my ways."

Aunt Rose looks thoughtful, and it makes me smile. She's a formidable lady when she wants to be, and I certainly wouldn't go up against her. Feeling a little brighter, I head to my room to grab my purse, but before I make the journey across town, there's something else I need to do first.

CHAPTER 24

SLADE

Most of the morning is spent digging up information on James Adams. Along with my men, we head around town, spreading the word and picking up any info we can. Now the words on the street, many are keen to talk and the manager at the Largo couldn't have been more helpful after we made it worth his while—by not trashing the place.

Marina sits with me and we spend the afternoon running through the information and by all accounts, this guy is lucky he hasn't been arrested. There are so many women he's taken to the Largo he must have paid the realty value of the place because he goes there at least four times a week and with a different girl each time.

"Man, he is something else."

Marina shakes her head as she reads through more papers. "What are you gonna do?"

"I know what I'd like to do."

She nods. "I'll lend a hand if you like—bastard."

She looks up and sighs. "He makes us look like angels because at least we stick to our own, people who know this life and want it. These girls think he's Prince Charming and fall in love with the creep. It's not right."

Her words make me think of Skye and picturing her in this world of sin we exist in, makes me feel better about setting her loose. It was like taking my own blade to my heart and carving it out because I have changed my mind a thousand times since then. I want her. I can't deny it. She's special, but the thought of her here—sharing my twisted life is almost as hard to bear as losing her. Women like Skye deserve more, and it would be selfish of me to try to make her do something she would regret a few years from now. Her happiness is all I want at the expense of my own.

"What's going on, Slade, you look as if—well, I've never seen you like this."

"Like what?"

Marina looks worried, "Well, so destroyed. I mean, is it Billy, are you thinking back to that night?"

"No, leave it, Marina."

I fix her with a dark look and she shakes her head. "You can pretend all you like, but something's not right. Sort it out, Slade, because if I know you, someone is about to pay big time for whatever evil thought is running through your mind. You know..." She brightens up. "I could help with that; you just have to say the word."

"No, Marina, I've told you, it's never gonna happen and for your information, I have rather a lot to deal with right now in case you've forgotten. Mainly that woman in the other room. Devon won't like where she's heading and I'm the fall guy."

"What do you mean? I thought..."

"Just leave, Marina, I need some time on my own to work this shit out."

She looks hurt, but I don't care about that. Marina hitting on me the whole time is yet another unwelcome problem, and so I need to get some space from her, Demi and the Dragons. It's like pressure on my heart and yet the only person I want to see right now would spit in my eye after how I treated her.

Grabbing my jacket and keys, I say roughly, "I'm heading out, call me if there's a problem."

"Where?"

"Out!"

I storm out, slamming the door behind me and wonder if I'll ever be happy. My life stretches before me with every day on repeat, and now I understand why my father kept his other life secret. When I heard that he was secretly married and planning to leave the club and travel with his wife, I couldn't believe what I was hearing. Nobody leaves the Dragons and certainly not for a woman. Billy was the president for Christ's sake and planning the unthinkable. Then he was murdered in his own office and that set off a chain of events that led to my uncle taking off traveling and my brother switching clubs, leaving me to pick up the pieces of something I'm not sure should be glued back together.

As I sit astride my Harley, I wonder if this is all worth it. Surely, I deserve better, but better is in the shape of only one woman and I have lost her for good. Just thinking about Skye makes me hard and yet it's not just the sex - it's her, the woman. The beautiful soul of an angel and the looks and body of one. I hope she will find her Prince, it's all I want.

Sighing, I reach for my helmet, but my attention switches to a car pulling into the yard. When I see who's come calling, I replace my helmet quickly and head to across to meet her. Rose. Billy's wife.

Before she can even park up, I hold up my hand and head to her window.

"What's up?"

"Nice to see you too, Slade."

She grins and my heart settles because she looks ok. I think my first thought was something had happened to Skye but by the looks of things, she's here for another reason.

"Can we talk?"

She looks worried and I nod. "Follow me."

As Rose parks up, I wait and as she walks toward me, she looks curious. "You know, Slade, I've never been to the Dragon's Ruin, can you believe that?"

"You weren't missing much; I expect Billy thought if you took one look at it, you'd never want to see him again."

She laughs. "You're probably right. He liked to keep his business separate from his private life, although I was always curious."

"If you're after a guided tour, it can be arranged."

"I think I'm good."

She smiles but I don't miss the anxiety in her expression and say quickly, "Come, I'll get Marina to make us a coffee, unless you fancy something stronger."

"Better not." She smiles. "I have to drive home and I'm working the bar later."

"Where's Skye?" I say it casually, but it's the only topic I want to talk about. Just saying her name is like shrugging on a cozy blanket and feeling it warm my soul.

"That's what I want to talk to you about."

I nod and turn away because I hope to God Skye never told her what I did because this woman's respect is something I'm keen to learn. Knowing I've already broken my promise to her would make a very bad day even worse.

CHAPTER 25

SKYE

The Coyote Bar. It looks exactly the same as the one I run with my aunt, but is more like home to me because this is where my parents live.

As soon as I head through the doors and see my mom's welcoming smile, I almost break down. She looks concerned and mumbles something to the girl working beside her and as I fall into her arms; they wrap around me shutting the whole world out.

"Hey, baby girl, you look as if you need your mom."

"I'm sorry, mom."

"Hush, whatever it is, we'll work it out. Now, come with me, it's been a long time since we spent some time together."

I follow her out the back and love the familiar sights of home. The bright open space of a kitchen that was re-modeled only last year and is open and warm. Family framed photographs showing a past that was filled with love and the familiar couch in front of the television, where all I want is to curl up and forget that I'm an adult and lose myself in comfort.

Mom smiles. "I'll fix us a drink, I'm due a break. This

place gets busier every day and we need more staff but don't have time to deal with it."

"Same." I sigh heavily and watch her make the drinks and she says brightly, "How's Rose? I keep on meaning to head over and take her out somewhere. She must be depressed just staying inside thinking on Billy."

"She's not good, mom. Hitting the whiskey hard and pretending it's all ok. What are we going to do about her?"

"*We* are not going to do anything, leave Rose to me."

"Why, how can you help her?"

"Be around more."

"But you just said you're too busy here, how will that work?"

"I've been thinking of swapping places with you; spend some time with Rose and by the looks of things, you could use the change of scene, what's the problem?"

"Can't you guess?"

"A man then." She looks almost hopeful.

"Have you met someone, what's he like?"

Just thinking of the look in her eyes change from hope to despair when she sees the man I've fallen completely and hopelessly in love with, makes me feel physically sick. They wouldn't understand. Dad is so straight he never even bends in the wind, and that's probably what I need in my life because they are the happiest people I know. Good, kind, loving human beings who wouldn't understand my choice. It was bad enough when Rose married Billy, mom was so worried and I would hate to be the person responsible for that look return, so I say sadly, "Have you ever had a dream, something so amazing you could think of nothing else?"

"Of course, I think most people have."

"Well, I've had one for a while now."

"A man?"

"Yes." She looks concerned and I sigh heavily.

"Well, I thought that dream had come true, but it turns out it wasn't worth the time."

"I'm sorry, baby, what happened?"

Deciding to spare her the gory details, I shrug. "Turns out I was just one in a line. A 'not so special after all' and when he took what he wanted, he shrugged me off like a dirty pair of pants and reached for a clean one."

Mom's eyes cloud with pain and she heads across and pulls me close. "I think I know what you're saying and I'm sorry, so sorry for that."

She strokes my hair and whispers, "You can't change what happened, but you can learn from it. Allow it to make you stronger and look for something better, *someone* better."

"What if I found that, but he doesn't feel the same? How do you deal with having one dream shatter over the previous one? How do you pick the pieces of your heart before it's healed from the last knock?"

"You don't. You let time heal it and carry on doing the things that bring you pleasure. Don't look for ways to make it better, let it happen naturally. You see, Skye, I'm not sure of the details but I'm guessing you were hurt and vulnerable and shifted your dreams onto the next man who caught your eye. It's natural, they call it a rebound, so maybe you should stop looking and let love find you."

I know deep in my heart Slade was no rebound. I didn't even like him when I asked him to teach me sex, and I still can't quite believe I did that. But he revealed a side to him that I fell in love with and that's the man I crave more than air, but when reality hit, he destroyed me in seconds. It's that feeling, that sense of finding someone so special you can't breathe without thinking of him and to have it snatched so cruelly away before it even had a chance to develop, is the cruelest of knocks.

Then there's the unwelcome attention from someone much like him, but worlds apart where it counts.

"You see, mom, my life is so complicated right now because there's also a third player in my story."

Mom actually laughs. "Lucky you."

"Not really, this guy would make Billy look like a priest."

"I see." Mom's tone changes in a heartbeat, and I sigh. "I'm not even interested, but he just won't take no for an answer. He's threatened to take up residence in the bar and scare away the customers unless I agree to be his woman. Can you believe the man, blackmailing me into his bed?"

Mom looks worried, and I feel bad for that.

"Should we call the cops?"

"Wouldn't work, he hasn't done anything wrong—yet. Then again, maybe I should take him up on his offer because I appear to messing things up on my own and my choices appear to be the wrong ones. Perhaps I should give him a chance and see where it leads."

"No!" Mom almost shouts, and I see the fierce look in her eye.

"Never settle for anything but the dream; I've always told you that. It's a long life with the wrong man. You know Skye, you're young and have so many years to find the right man. It may seem difficult now, but nature has a way of working it all out. Give it time and don't settle for anything less than fantastic. In the meantime, I'll take your place in the bar for a few weeks and you can work with your father and nobody would dare go up against him. Take some time to think, sort yourself out, and then we'll talk again."

"That's not fair on you, or dad."

"He'll live." She winks. "And I'll get some girly time with Rose. Maybe the guy will lose interest and move onto the next girl when you're not around."

"We can only hope." I smile, feeling as if a weight has shifted. "Thanks, mom, I knew you'd make me feel better."

I spend the rest of the day catching up with my parents and already feel tons better. I'm not sure if it will work but it's worth a try and at least I wouldn't be nervous every time the door opened, expecting to see one of the three men who have ruined everything walk inside. This is just what I need, so as I head home to pack my bags and square it with Rose, I do so with a smile on my face.

CHAPTER 26

SLADE

It feels strange seeing Rose here. Sitting behind Billy's desk because that was the first thing she'd asked. She looks emotional as she runs her hands over the leather chair and has a faraway look in her eyes.

"I can see him here." She appears wistful, and for some reason I have a lump in my throat as I watch her from across the room. I never saw them together when he was alive, hell I never even knew she existed and I wish I had. I wish he'd trusted his secret to me because I would have liked to see him happy. After mom died, any happiness we had as a family died with her and I suppose that's why I fell into the darkness and have struggled to find my way out.

"I can feel him around me, it's as if he's here."

She looks at me with large eyes that are brimming with tears and I say gruffly, "Yes, Billy belonged in this office. It's hard not to see him sitting there, taking charge and making it all better. It's a lot to live up to."

She fixes me with a look that makes me stand a little taller and smiles, "You will be a great successor. You're his son and if anything, you have his blood in your veins, so how can you be anything but magnificent."

Her words strike me hard and for a moment, a little emotion finds its way into my soul and it could be Skye sitting there, staring at me through those eyes that believe in me. Skye is much like her aunt and I say sadly, "Do you ever wish Billy had opened up about you and brought you here to live?"

She nods. "Yes, it's my main regret that I never got to see the whole of him." She sighs. "You see, Slade, I loved your father with a passion that had no conditions attached. Billy hid our secret because he feared for our safety. He didn't want us to be targeted by the Dragon's enemies, but I knew it was more than that. He was afraid that I wouldn't look at him the same way if I saw him here. That I couldn't cope with the man he had to be when he ran this club and that I couldn't live this life. I suppose he had good reason, after all, it broke your mom."

She shakes her head and looks concerned. "It's enough to break anyone, but he was wrong."

"Why?"

"Because I loved him and that, as they say, conquers all. Looking back, we wasted so much time that we could have spent together. What was the use of hiding when his time was limited, as it turned out? Maybe if I had been here, he would never have been shot. Perhaps circumstances would have changed and well, I know that's just wishful thinking but all I know is that when you find the man you were supposed to love, nothing should get in the way of that."

A sharp knock on the door interrupts us and Marina heads inside, balancing a tray with some coffee, and she looks at Rose with curiosity.

"I brought you this, although I can make it a stronger beverage if you prefer."

She smiles and Rose laughs softly, "I would prefer but I won't. The coffee is fine. Thank you."

Marina hesitates and I suppose, like me, she is curious about the woman whose life is tangled up with ours but unknown to us and I say sharply, "Thanks, Marina."

I stare at the door and she nods and then turns to Rose and smiles. "I'm sorry for your loss. I never knew Billy that well, but I know his family and he must have been one amazing guy. You were very lucky."

Rose nods. "I was, even though we had so little time by anyone else's standards, it was worth a lifetime because I wouldn't change a moment of it except the end."

She smiles and I see the tears sparkling in her eyes as Marina nods. "I'll leave you to talk."

Rose sips her coffee and waits for her footsteps to die away and then says with a determination that shows she means business. "I came to ask a favor."

Grabbing the chair opposite the desk, I sit and regard her coolly. "It's yours."

"You don't even know what it is."

"It could be anything, you are family."

For a moment, she seems shaken by that and I watch her take a deep breath and a small smile ghosts her face. "I suppose I am."

She takes another sip and for all her front, I can see she is struggling. "We have a problem."

"I'm listening."

"Skye seems to have attracted some unwelcome attention."

I stiffen at the mention of Skye and wonder if that attention means me, and yet thinking of her as anything but safe has stirred the beast inside me.

"Go on." I am struggling to maintain my cool as she sighs heavily. "The president of the Dark Lords."

I say nothing but my fists clench as I think of Devon anywhere near Skye and I don't miss that Rose is watching me keenly for my reaction. I don't give her one and say roughly, "What's he done?"

"Nothing—yet."

I relax a little. "It's what he wants to do that worries me."

She leans back and watches me closely. "Skye is a beautiful woman and innocent in many ways. For years she's held an obsession for a man she always placed on a pedestal. For some reason, he appears to have fallen off that and she's lost. Her confidence in her judgment has been dented, and I suppose that is why she agreed to go out on a date with him."

"She went on a date with Devon Santiago." I say every word slowly as if I can't believe them and say roughly, "When?"

"Last night. I'm not sure what, but something happened to Skye, and she went away for a bit and returned with a desperate look in her eye. She looked even more troubled than when she went, and all the fight seemed to have left her. Perhaps that's why she agreed to go out with him at all and when she returned, she looked even more destroyed. She told me he wants her to be his girl and until she agrees, he will move his club into the Coyote Bar and scare away our customers. He's not taking no for an answer and she seems so unlike herself, I'm worried she'll give in."

She looks at me with a hopeful expression.

"That's why I came to you. For your help, any ideas?"

Just thinking of Devon anywhere near Skye is sending a murderous rage to my heart, but this isn't that straightforward. I have his sister currently waiting on leaving this club and for all he knows, I'm about to make her my old lady. I can't lay any claim to Skye and I can't let on Rose has any connection to my family because that would make Billy return and haunt me from his grave. He spent his time protecting her from club shit and at the first chance I get, I would drag her into it.

I feel so frustrated I'm finding it hard to think and just say roughly, "Where's Skye now?"

Just saying her name wraps me in happiness and I wonder how I fell so deeply for a woman I should avoid like the plague.

"I sent her home, to be with her parents. She's safe for now and when he comes calling tonight, she won't be there, but we both know that tactic won't last long. He'll be back and won't stop until she agrees to go with him."

"What do you want me to do?" I'm curious as to what she's thinking, and she looks worried.

"I want you to move in."

CHAPTER 27

SKYE

I feel more upbeat as I make my way home. My parents are good for that. Mom is always there to put me back on the right path and dad is the strong but silent type who asks no questions, never judges and just makes everything better with a look, a smile and a promise in his eyes. He is always there for me, as is my whole family, which is why it's so important to me to make the right choices myself.

Devon is the wrong choice. I know that; I don't even like him, but he's the only one interested. The one I am most interested in couldn't make it more obvious if he tried that it's completely one sided. And then there's James; what a disappointment he turned out to be. Nothing like I imagined during all those years of yearning, lustful looks and hopes for a future with him, which is why it's a surprise when I pull up to see him heading toward my car.

Immediately, I tense up, despite the fact he's smiling and looking at me so apologetically, I have a moment's hesitation before saying angrily, as I slam my car door shut, "Get out of here, you're not welcome."

"I'm sorry, Skye, you have every right to be angry."

"You think!"

I throw him my most disinterested look and he nods. "I deserve that, to be honest, I deserve so much more but I'm worried about you."

"You needn't, I'm nothing to do with you."

I make to walk away and he grabs my arm and says firmly, "Hear me out."

Making to shrug him off, he grips me harder and says in an even voice, "I know you're angry and I respect that, I would be in your position but hear me out, it's important."

"Ok, two minutes."

Sighing, I turn to face him and hate the look he's giving me because it's one I have imagined in my dreams for the past few years. He smiles and his eyes dance with desire—for me and yet there's something else, a familiarity, a sense of destiny and for some reason, I relax my guard a little.

"Can we start again?"

"I wasn't aware there was a *we*."

He nods. "I'd like there to be."

"It's a bit late for that. Why now?"

He runs his fingers through his hair and smiles ruefully. "I've been uncomfortable about what happened between us. I felt bad leaving you like that, when I should have wrapped you in my arms and told you I loved you. Maybe I panicked, I'm not sure why I left in such a hurry, I suppose because I was scared of my feelings for you."

"Is that right?" I'm cynical for a reason, and he winces a little.

"I deserve your coldness, I brought that on myself, when all you have ever been is so sweet and kind. A girl I couldn't ignore who turned into a woman I want to get to know better. Maybe take things slowly and build a relationship together."

He laughs nervously. "I can't believe I'm saying that because I've never wanted one before, but it took losing the chance with you to make me see what a fool I was. You gave me your most important treasure, and I blew it. I should have taken you out for dinner, wined and dined you and made it count. Not a quick one in a bar. You deserve more than that and I'd like the chance to make up for my mistake and start again. Treat you right this time, if you'll let me, that is."

The fact I'm even considering this right now shows me I am right to get away. I need a break from it all and so I say wearily, "I appreciate that, but I'm need of some space to think. I'm heading off for a couple of weeks and have just come back for my things. Maybe you should call back when I return and I'll think on what you said."

"Where are you going?" He looks a little panicked.

"Is it with him, the man I saw you with last night, the biker?"

"No, would it matter if it was?"

"Yes, Skye, it would matter a great deal. You see the moment I saw you with another guy, I knew."

"What?"

"That I didn't want to let you go, let the opportunity slip for us to be a couple. All those years of staring at you across the classroom meant something in that instant. It meant that we were destined to be together and the first opportunity I got, I messed it up. That man isn't right for you. Not a delicate, innocent, beautiful woman like you."

"And you are, I suppose."

He steps closer and stares at me with a look that I have craved since the moment I met him. "Yes, Skye, I am. Let's not waste any more time, let me make it up to you and who knows where it might lead? I have a good job, can provide a nice home, a comfortable life and will make it my business to treat you like a princess, my princess, so what do you say, give us a chance?"

I am so tempted right now because James is offering me everything I wanted since I first saw him. It has always been him, always James, and thinking on how good it could be, makes me almost believe in miracles. Then again, I've seen a different side to him since then, a side I dislike with a passion and I'm no fool. He may have the right words, but I can see the future and it wouldn't be as rosy as he paints it to be.

There would be other women, lots of women, and I would always be wondering where he was and who with. He's already shown himself to be a man I can't trust, and yet, I'm so weary inside. If I could choose anyone, it would be the man who should be the last one on my list, instead of what society would deem the most suitable, who is standing in front of me offering me everything I ever wanted.

Fixing a small smile on my face, I say gently, "It sounds so tempting and I will definitely think about it. Maybe when I get back, we can revisit this conversation."

I turn to go and his hand grabs mine and squeezes it hard. "Before you do, come and have dinner with me. Let me spend some time with you."

I snatch my hand away. "No, James, I told you, I need space and I need to get on the road. Look, it was good of you to come here, but I really don't have time for this."

Once again, I turn to go and as I step away from the man who could have been my world, I feel a sharp pain and then everything goes blank.

CHAPTER 28

SLADE

That was the last thing I thought she'd say, and she looks worried.

"I know it's a strange request, but I thought if the president of The Dark Lords thought you were, um with Skye, he would stay away."

"No."

I'm abrupt and I hate hearing the anger in my tone because she flinches a little and says hesitantly, "You won't help us."

I am battling so hard inside because I want her niece more than anything but I promised her I would stay away and living under the same roof as the woman I can't appear to shake from my heart, would have me breaking my promise before my bags were unpacked.

"But why?"

"I can't because God help me, I've got Devon Santiago's sister under my roof and he thinks I'm about to make her my old lady."

Rose looks shocked. "I didn't know."

"Neither did I." I laugh bitterly.

"She told him I'd fucked her up badly, and he wants me to make an honest woman of her, or burn my club to the ground. What was I supposed to do?"

"And did you?"

"Not that night."

She looks shocked and I shrug. "I'm a bastard, Rose, it's why you warned me off your niece. I've been out of control for so long, I've forgotten what it's like to be a decent person. The women love it, the harder the better. Every girl loves a bad boy it seems, and that gives me a license to be a bastard."

"Not every girl."

Rose looks at me with a determined glint in her eye.

"Not every girl loves a bad boy, Slade. You may hide behind a reputation and use it to make what you do acceptable. The women who let you, crave the image, the protection, the trophy. Not a real woman. Not a woman who accepts your flaws and loves you despite them. Not someone who makes your heart double the size and a better person for letting them in. Don't you think Billy was a bastard? He was. He was crude, rough and violent at times, but never to me. You see, love has a habit of teaching a person what matters and if you truly love someone, you will do everything in your power to keep them safe, to never harm them and wish like crazy you never cause them pain. Billy loved me, Slade, he wasn't that man with me and when you find the right woman, you won't need anything more than her love to make you happy. You will move Heaven and Earth for her, which is what Billy did for me. He denied us our present to protect our future. How ironic is that? So, when you find your true love, fight for her and don't let yourself be forced down a path you are reluctant to step on. If you don't want to marry this woman, stand up to her brother and tell him. Whatever he does can't be worse than lying to yourself, to her either. She deserves better than that and it would make me so proud if you found the courage to be true to yourself because as sure as Devon Santiago wants my niece, no one else is going to do it for you."

She stands and says sadly, "I like you, Slade, I see a lot of Billy in you, the trouble is, you don't. You see only the bad and let it control you. I came because I trust you, for some strange reason I do, and the man I warned to stay away from my niece is the person you are now, not the one I know you are deep inside. Anyway, I've taken up enough of your time because I can see that you have problems of your own. It was worth a shot at least, but hey, we'll figure a way out of this, I mean, Skye's a strong woman and I think perfectly capable of sending this biker packing. It just may take a little time to get him to accept it."

She heads to the door and then stops and takes another last lingering look at the office. "I can see Billy here. It smells of him. Leather, whiskey, and loyalty. There's nothing better in my opinion, if only he realized that."

She smiles ruefully and heads outside, leaving me feeling like the biggest bastard in the world. Then again, how can I stake my claim on something I want more than life itself when everyone around me is intent on ruining my life and I won't be responsible for doing the same to Skye?

∽

IT MUST BE an hour later I get a call that changes everything.

"Hey, what's up, Gibbs?"

"I'm at the Largo as we agreed, staking it out and that fuckers just checked in with another girl."

"Bastard, so why are you calling me?"

"Because this one seems out of it. Normally they walk in all giggly and keen. This one appears drugged, and he is holding her up, but she's out cold. I snapped a picture; I'm sending it through."

He cuts the call and as I wait, I think of that bastard and wonder why he does this. Surely, he's one step away from a sex offender and as the picture comes through, I think my heart shatters into a million pieces because the woman he is holding up is Skye.

Grabbing my jacket, I call him back.

"I'm on my way. If I'm not there in ten minutes, break the fucking door down."

As I storm out of the office, Marina races after me. "What's happening?"

"No time."

I call to a couple of the guys smoking outside. "Follow me."

Shouting to Marina, I say angrily, "Tell the rest of them to meet me at the Largo, now."

She runs inside and as I fire up my Harley, I have murder on my mind.

∼

I'M THERE in seven minutes. We pull up beside Gibbs and I snarl, "What room?"

"Second floor, third one in."

I nod and say roughly, "Call the cops."

"Are you sure?"

"Do it."

I take off and shout to my men, "Follow me."

I run like crazy to get to Skye before that bastard hurts her and don't think twice and kick the door in, and before he can even blink, I punch the bastard full in the face.

He groans, and it feels good to hear the bone crack and see the blood spilling across his wasted face and as he's on the ground, I direct a sharp kick to his balls, relishing his screams. Then I snarl to my men, "Tie him to the chair."

As they drag him off, I turn my attention to the heap on the bed and growl in anger as I see he was in the process of tying her arms and legs to the bed. The rage consumes me when I think about what he had in mind for her and my heart breaks as I see the woman I love, drugged and out cold, not knowing what she just escaped.

The sirens wail in the distance and it takes all my self-restraint not to touch her right now and as my men look on and the teacher sobs, I wait for something alien to me - to do the right thing.

CHAPTER 29

SLADE

The cops arrive and tell us to kneel and put our hands on our heads and it pains me to see them deal with Skye by untying her and calling for an ambulance.

Once they have secured our weapons, the cop in charge looks around and whistles. "Who's first?"

I speak up. "I can tell you everything you need to know."

Luckily, Skye is still out cold and knows none of this, and as I fill the cop in, I watch as the medics arrive and tend to her with more care than I could.

"She's been drugged, she'll be out cold, but not for long. We'll take her to the hospital for observation."

The cop nods. "I'll send one of my men with her. When she wakes, we'll get her statement."

It physically hurts as I see her put on a stretcher and carried off to the waiting ambulance without me by her side. I have to do this the right way though because I will not let the teacher walk away from this.

As soon as they leave, the cop says angrily, "Start talking."

James shouts, "Arrest them, officer, they came in and

attacked me and tied up my girlfriend and told me they were going to…" He breaks off sobbing.

"I thought they were going to rape her and kill us both. I told them to leave but well, look at them."

My men growl and I say darkly, "Keep telling yourself that, we have enough evidence to bury you, you fucker and this time you can't hide."

The cop looks interested. "What evidence?"

I hold up my cuffed hands and say wearily, "I want to do this properly. It's why I called you. This man has been getting away with this for too long and this time he messed with the wrong woman."

"Is she your…"

I nod and James laughs. "And every other biker out there. She was with a different one last night, don't make me laugh."

I make to grab him and the officers pull me down sharply. "Get him out of here." The cop is angry, and yet it's not me he's referring to. Instead, they haul James to his feet and as he protests, they manhandle him out of the room. The cop looks at the three of us and sighs. "It's ok, we know about him."

"You do?" I stare at him in shock as he sits on the bed and shakes his head. "We have a file on him that's growing by the day. Many girls have filed complaints against him, but until now, there's not been enough evidence. What made you call us; don't bikers take care of their own shit?"

"Yes, we do." I stare at him with a hard expression.

"This wasn't about me, my club, or him. It was about Skye and all the women and young girls that bastard has messed with. It would be easy to take matters in my own hands, but I want it done right. If he walks, then maybe he won't be so lucky next time, but I'm not about to do time over a loser like that, I have more important things to do."

The cop nods respectfully. "I'm glad to hear it. Send me in

your evidence and we'll add it to the file. You did the right thing; he's not getting away that easily and with the young ladies' statement, it will help put him in orange quicker than you can get to your woman's side."

"Does that mean?"

"You're free to go. All of you."

He nods to the other cop standing guard. "Un-cuff them, then we need to take prints and photograph the room for evidence."

As we make to leave, he calls out. "I appreciate your help; I owe you one."

I just nod and leave, feeling something strange inside. For some reason, it felt good doing the right thing for once. Leaving it to the cops to deal with the trash. I wasn't lying when I said I wouldn't do time for that man because the only thing I'm intent on doing is securing mine and Skye's future and that's just where I'm heading now.

∽

I SEND my men back to the Castle and head straight for the hospital. I can't get there quickly enough and as I ride, I think about how things have changed. It's obvious Skye can't be trusted out on her own, and rather than saving her from trouble, I'm placing her deeper into it and she's struggling. For all my best intentions, I'm fast realizing the safest place for Skye Slater is by my side and I just hope she agrees to that.

I park up and know I must be an intimidating sight as I storm through the double doors in full club leathers, with a death stare fixed on anyone that looks my way. I head to the nearest nurse and say roughly, "Skye Slater, where is she?"

The nurse fixes me with a disapproving look. "You'll have to take a seat."

"But…"

"Now. I don't care who you think you are, but this is a hospital and we have procedures. Sit down."

I don't miss the smirks thrown in my direction and I lean in and say with a dark hiss, "Listen, I don't give a shit about your procedures and I'm pretty certain you don't want to see me when I'm angry, so do us both a favor and tell me where I can find my woman because she is probably scared shitless right now and needs me."

I'm not sure if it's because she can't wait to see the back of me, is scared of me, or sees the brightness in my eyes as I mention Skye, but she says in a softer voice, "Follow me."

We head down the hall and she says firmly, "She has two police officers with her, just to warn you."

"I know, I called them." She looks surprised and I say roughly, "I know what you're thinking and it wasn't me. That's why I'm so keen to get to her. You would too if someone you loved had been drugged and kidnapped by a sex predator."

She looks shocked and I nod. "So, I'm sorry if I'm a little on edge, but I think I have good reason."

We reach a room with two cops standing outside and she says quickly, "She's in there. I'll go and see if she's up to visitors."

Leaving me with the cops, she heads inside and I say nothing and just lean against the wall and feel the frustration tearing me up inside. I can't concentrate on anything but holding her in my arms and making sure she's ok.

It doesn't take long before the nurse opens the door. "You can go in now."

The cops look up and she says firmly, "Just him. You'll get your statement when she's good and ready."

One of the cops looks angry. "I'm sorry ma'am but this a

police inquiry. This man's involved and we need to make sure he doesn't tamper with the witness."

"For fuck's sake..." I growl and the nurse sighs.

"Then one of you can go in as well. Two minutes and then I'm coming back; she's been through a trauma and doesn't need this on top of it."

Fixing the cop with my darkest look, I head inside and he follows, but he may as well be invisible because the only thing I can focus on is the woman looking so vulnerable in the hospital bed, who blinks when she sees me coming.

"Slade." Her voice is soft and hesitant and I see her beautiful blue eyes swimming with tears. In two strides, I reach her and pull her hard against me, not even considering if she agrees or not. I hold her head against my chest and feel a surge of love for this woman and say gruffly, "I can't leave you for a minute."

She sobs into my chest and her arms fold around me and pull me closer and as I stroke her hair, I whisper, "It's ok, darlin', I've got you."

The cop clears his throat. "Excuse me, Miss. Slater."

"Can't you just..."

I make to speak and Skye pulls back and says softly, "It's ok, Slade, let him speak."

She grips me hard and I shift next to her on the bed, putting my arm around her shoulders and pulling her close to me. Now I have her in my arms, I'm not keen to let her go and she doesn't appear to mind about that and says to the cop, "I'm sorry I don't have much I can tell you. One minute I was talking to James Adams in the car park of the Coyote Bar and then, as I turned away, I felt a sharp pain in my neck. Then I woke up here. What happened?"

Her voice shakes as she probably fears the worst and the cop writes it all down and then says kindly, "I think you had a lucky escape. We were called to the Largo hotel and found you tied up in one of the rooms. Mr. Adams was also tied up and beaten badly, and this man and two others were there too."

"You were there." She looks at me through wide eyes and I nod.

"We had a tail on him ever since that night in the bar. We've been gathering evidence on him and when Gibbs called and told me he had just dragged an unconscious girl into a room at the Largo, I came running because he also sent me a photo and I recognized you immediately."

"What did you find?" Her voice is tearful and I smile reassuringly. "He was tying you to the bed, and you were out cold. I hit the bastard and waited for the cops."

"But why call them?" Her eyes are wide and I shrug.

"I wanted to do it right. Where you're concerned, darlin', I always want to do the right thing. No messing around, no cut corners, just what's right—for you."

She stares at me in amazement and her eyes sparkle with unshed tears, but before she can answer, the cop coughs nervously. "You say he sent you a picture, may I take a look?"

Nodding, I scroll to it and hand him my phone and he nods. "You did well to request this. It's evidence and also puts you in the clear. Good job."

He takes my phone and puts it in a clear bag and seals it and I say angrily, "What the…"

He winks. "You'll get it back; I need to add it to the evidence on the case. I should be in a position to get it back to you by the morning at the latest."

He stands and shakes his head. "It was fortunate he was around, Miss. Slater; you had a lucky escape. Well, I'll be leaving now, unless you need us to stay, for protection, or a ride home."

"I've got it." I glare at him and he looks at Skye. "Miss. Slater."

She says quickly, "Thanks, officer, for everything."

"Just doing my job." As he closes the door softly behind him, I turn and look into the most beautiful eyes in the world and say gently, "I'm sorry, darlin'."

"What for?"

"For leaving you in the first place. I should have known you couldn't be trusted on your own, and now you have no choice."

"What choice?"

"You're stuck with me."

Leaning down, I touch my lips to hers and know I've made the right decision. We may be involved in a shit storm right now, but we will get through it the right way and together.

CHAPTER 30

SKYE

I feel as if I'm still dreaming. Am I really awake? Is Slade really here, holding me so tenderly and making everything better almost immediately? Just feeling his hands on me, his lips tasting mine and his body beside me, is enough for me to know it's only him, will only ever be him and it appears that he feels the same.

I kiss him back so fiercely, I think it shocks him a little but I can't help that and as I slide my hands under his t-shirt, I am desperate to feel his skin against mine. His kiss deepens and I shift closer and as his fingers tangle my hair and pulls me in closer, we hear an angry, "Stop that at once, this is a hospital and this woman is sick."

The nurse looks at Slade with tightly controlled fury and I giggle. "I'm sorry, I was just so pleased to see..."

"Her old man." He fills in the words and they fill my heart with butterflies. His old lady, but...

"Are you sure about that?" I stare at him with a hard look. "I thought you already had one."

"I'm still here."

The nurse sounds angry, but Slade completely ignores her. "Who told you that?"

"Devon."

"Excuse me."

"Oh, yes, we need to have the Devon conversation. What the fuck were you thinking going out with him last night?"

"Because you left me."

"Hello, anybody listening?"

The nurse sounds even more annoyed and Slade groans. "For your own good. I left you to protect you from our world, you deserve more, not to run off with the next biker who asks."

"But…"

"Enough, I'm leaving now because god help me, I've got better things to be doing right now, so sort your shit out and come and find me when you're ready to go."

She turns and slams the door behind her and Slade says gruffly, "I was protecting you. You need better than me, better than Devon, and definitely better than James in your life. You don't need to be involved in our shit and I was cutting you loose for your own protection."

"What if I didn't want to be cut loose? What if I wanted to be tied to you because there was nowhere else I'd rather be? You never gave me that choice, you never asked what I wanted."

"Because I was doing what was best for you." He sounds angry, which makes me annoyed. "There's no need to shout, you know. You don't get to tell me what's right for me, I can make my own decisions."

"Like riding out with Devon fucking Santiago, good decision I might add, way to go, nailed that one."

He leans in and says angrily, "Did you kiss him?"

"Yes."

He exhales sharply and I groan. "What did you expect, I

was angry? He told me you were making his sister your old lady, and I thought… Anyway, I kissed him out of revenge. A revenge kiss that I wish I could say was sweet, but quite frankly that man makes my skin crawl and…"

He cuts off my words by claiming my lips and kissing the hell out of me. He doesn't stop there and fists my hair and grinds into me as I fight for breath. His kiss lights a fuse so intense I'm burning for him and his hands run under my top and as I feel his touch, it sends me wild.

Then we hear loud voices outside and the nurse saying, "I really wouldn't go in there if I were you."

We quickly pull back and as the door opens, I think I'm in shock as Aunt Rose storms inside the room and fixes us both with a hard look.

"And what exactly is going here?"

Slade leans back and to my surprise, he smiles and my aunt's fierce looks softens in an instant, as he says, "I'm moving in."

∾

I'm surprised to see my aunt with Slade. They have an easy friendship that I never knew about. We filled her in and she was shocked and concerned, but I think she knew immediately that Slade was more than just a friend and I know I have some explaining to do.

Luckily, she brought her car and after finding the nurse, we head off and Slade says, "I'll head back to the Castle and pick up the evidence and drop it to the station. Then I'll meet you at the bar, so when Devon comes calling later, I'll be ready."

He nods to my aunt. "I'm sorry, Rose, you probably have a few questions for me but they will have to wait."

"It's fine, I think we'll have time for those later. Over a whiskey perhaps, you make a good drinking partner."

"Nobody will be drinking tonight. We have a lot to deal with." I pretend to be annoyed, but how can I be? Two of my favorite people in the world, obviously comfortable with each other. That means the world to me and as my aunt unlocks the car, I step into Slade's arms and whisper, "Are you sure about this?"

He leans down and says huskily, "More than anything, you're my girl, Skye, whether you like it or not."

"Oh, I like it, biker. I like it a lot."

Completely forgetting that my aunt is watching, I kiss Slade slowly, with a promise that this is just our beginning and I can't wait to see what comes next.

As soon as he leaves, my aunt makes sure I'm settled in the car before she joins me and as she starts the engine, she laughs softly, "I never saw that coming."

"Didn't you? From what I heard, you warned him off."

"Yes, I did." She laughs. "Typical biker, didn't listen to a word I said."

"Does that bother you?"

"Not really. If he's half the man his father was, you made the right decision."

"Only half?"

"Yes, nobody can measure up to that man, he was one of a kind."

Once again, I feel my aunt's pain as she talks about her husband and I'm starting to understand how devastated she must be feeling. Reaching out, I take her hand and squeeze it hard. "I'm sorry."

"What for, Billy, or Slade?"

"Billy, of course." I laugh. "You know, I never intended on falling for Slade Channing. He kind of worked his way into my heart, and I blinked one day and saw him there. He is so different to what I thought. Kind, caring, loving and... well, you know."

I giggle and my aunt grins. "Trust me, honey, I know. Anyway, you can fill me in on the journey home, but not before you tell me you're ok. When the cops came to the bar, I almost joined Billy in the grave. I thought something had happened, but even I never expected that."

"I was such a fool. Why didn't I see how damaged that man is?"

"Sometimes we only see the bad in appearance. We don't look behind that before we judge. Your teacher was an outwardly respectable man. He wore fine clothes and hid his depravity behind a smile. Sometimes the one who makes a woman's soul shiver, is actually hiding a heart of an angel and teaches us both one thing, never judge a book by its cover."

"Oh, I don't know, I think Slade's soul is pretty damned dark but there's a little light there and now the cracks have appeared, hopefully it won't be long before it breaks and lets the light flood the darkness."

"Not too much though, a girl likes a little shade in her life."

My aunt laughs out loud and I stare at her in shock. Who is this woman?

CHAPTER 31

SLADE

The first person I see when I return is Demi. She's outside smoking and sitting on the step and smiles as I pull up. "Hey, baby, did you miss me?"

"No."

I fling my helmet on the bike and say wearily, "Change of plan. I'm telling your brother tonight."

Her eyes flash. "Why?"

"Because I'm sick of being manipulated. We both know I don't deserve this and yes, we have history but it was one night only. I have other more important things to do and I'm telling you now, so you can make other arrangements because if things go according to plan, your brother will be where I'm standing later on tonight and he'll be taking you with him."

"Why, I thought we had an understanding?"

She looks so upset it softens my heart a little because despite everything, Demi and I are friends. Fucked-up friends with benefits but I understand her, we're two of a kind and I don't want to see her hurt.

"Listen, darlin', how you get your kicks is up to you, I'm

not one to judge but Devon, he's your brother, he cares about you. If I had a sister, I would tear the world apart to find her if she was in danger, and I kind of think you will be if you go off with this guy. It's a shit world out there, and getting involved with the mafia isn't one of your best decisions. So, head home and make peace with your brother, or expect a visitor later on tonight. I'm giving you fair warning because of what we've been through together but I can't be a part of this, it doesn't sit right with me."

She looks as if she's about to cry and flicks her cigarette to the ground and heads my way. She wraps her arms around me and lays her head on my chest and whispers, "I love you, Slade, you're my only friend around here and if circumstances, had been different, maybe things could have worked out for us. It would certainly be one fucked-up kind of marriage, but I'm guessing the woman who claims your heart will a very special one indeed."

Reaching up, she kisses me softly on the lips and then pulls away. "Thanks for the warning, I'll think on it."

I watch her head inside and I hope she's still here when Devon comes calling, for her sake.

∽

Marina is cleaning the office when I make it there and smiles. "Hey, I was wondering where you were, the guys came back hours ago, do you fancy something to eat, or maybe something else?"

Once again, she flashes me a hopeful look and I say softly, "Listen, Marina, I just want to say you have a home here for as long as you need it. That's all though. A job and a home; a family of sorts, but not me. I'm sorry if I give you the wrong signals, but I'm moving on and cleaning up my act."

"You're leaving?" Marina's eyes are wide.

"Of course not." I laugh as I shake my head.

"I will never leave the Dragons. No, I'm taking an old lady."

"Demi? I thought…"

"Not Demi."

I have never seen pain in a woman's eyes like I see now in Marina's and it's hard to watch when a woman's heart breaks and shines out through her devastated eyes.

"Who is she?" Her voice shakes and has a husky edge to it and I say gently, "The woman on my bike the other day. Skye Slater. She runs the Coyote Bar with her aunt."

"Billy's wife, Rose?"

Marina looks shocked and I nod. "Yes, Skye is, well, she's everything to me and that is something I never thought I'd find. I certainly don't deserve a woman like her, but for some reason, she sees past the shit and still likes me."

Marina looks worried. "Is she moving in, to the Castle?"

"No, she lives and works in the bar. Like Billy, I will head over there when I can and yes, I suppose she will spend some time here because unlike Billy, I intend on spending every night with her."

Marina sobs and sits down hard. "She's a lucky girl."

"Not really, you see, I'm not such a great catch, darlin'. There is someone way better than me out there for you. It's just that I'm Skye's man, whether she wanted that or not. Sometimes love blinds us to what we want or need over what we crave. You think you want me, but not really. When you find the perfect man, you will understand but until then, make Skye welcome here because I won't have it any other way."

She nods and says in a sad voice, "Be happy, Slade, you deserve it you know and despite how much I wish it was me, I want you to be happy, both of you."

She sighs. "Anyway, I should be getting to the bar. We're

still looking for that bartender, you know. I can't think why no one's applied."

"Really, I can think of several."

I manage to get a small smile from her before she heads to the door, leaving me with yet another feeling of guilt. This is not great but when you do the right thing, it doesn't always feel good at the time but is better in the long term.

∽

GRABBING the file on James from my desk, I head to my room and pack an overnight bag. As I head out, I see Gibbs and nod. "Good work today, keep it up."

He nods. "It felt good to see justice done the right way for once, how's the girl?"

"She's fine." A broad smile breaks across my face and he blinks in surprise because it's probably the first time he's seen it.

"You know, Gibbs, I have a good feeling about the future. We can make this work and make this a club my daddy and Axel would be proud of. So, I was thinking, I want you to be my deputy, is that ok with you?"

His eyes widen and he looks at me with rare emotion on his face and nods. "I'd be honored."

"Good, then you can start by keeping watch on the Castle tonight. I'm staying away, but I'll be back in the morning."

"Can I ask where?"

"Of course, the Coyote Bar. In fact, when I'm not here, I'll mainly be there, so get used to it."

He nods and as I turn to leave, says gruffly, "I'm happy for you man."

"Me too, brother, me too."

∽

THE COYOTE BAR is busy as usual and I have to push my way inside. I don't miss the anxious looks thrown in my direction and I know I'm an intimidating figure in my club leathers and shoulder length hair. I rarely shave, and the scar running across my eye tells people not to mess with me. Skye is nowhere to be seen, and neither is Rose, but a woman who looks very much Skye is serving behind the bar and I guess at once it's her mom.

She glares at me as I approach the bar and says curtly, "Can I help you?"

"I'm here to see Skye."

"She's not here."

I'm wondering if anyone told her what's happening because this woman couldn't be any more unwelcome if she tried.

"Listen, I'm sorry, but I kind of know she is and you may not like the look of me but I was invited here by Rose."

"Rose asked you?" She looks surprised and I nod.

"So, you're not Devon?"

A flash of irritation in my expression must tell her what she needs to know, and she looks at me with curiosity, "Then who are you?"

"Slade Channing, Dragon's Ruin."

I see the realization hit her and she gasps, "Billy's son?"

"Yes."

She looks upset. "I'm sorry for your loss."

"Thanks."

For a moment it's awkward and then she sighs. "I expect you've come to see Rose."

Thinking it best not to ruin her day even more, I nod. "Is she out the back?"

"Yes, I'll call her."

She heads off and I wonder if she'll accept me in her daughter's life. I know Rose will because she knows us, she doesn't see the reputation but the men behind it. I wonder if Skye's mother will give me that chance.

She heads back and her smile's a little friendlier.

"You can go through. Oh, and Slade…"

I look up and see an apology in her eyes. "I'm sorry for my frosty welcome, I thought…"

"That I was Devon, I'm nothing like him."

She nods and lets me pass and I wonder what the night will bring because this is not going to down well with him.

CHAPTER 32

SKYE

It felt good to be home and even better when I saw my mom waiting. Apparently, as soon as Rose got the call, she alerted my parents and mom was luckily on her way.

Now, as mom takes my place in the bar and Rose fusses around me in the kitchen, it feels so good to be me. Mainly though, because Slade is on his way here, and I still can't wrap my head around the fact he wants me. How did that happen? I woke from a nightmare to find all my dreams come true. Not that he's your typical Prince Charming, but he's mine.

As soon as my aunt smiles, I know he's here as she looks up from the counter and smiles in that special way she appears only to reserve for him.

He heads straight across and crouches down before me, looking concerned. "How are you feeling?"

"I'm good thanks." I smile shyly because for some reason he makes me feel that way. Despite what we've shared, I still don't know him inside and out, and I wonder what he's thinking right now.

He stares deep into my eyes and it shuts the whole world out. Then he says, "Your mom hates me."

Aunt Rose laughs. "I would be surprised if she didn't."

Slade sits beside me on the couch and puts his arms around my shoulder and pulls me close, as Aunt Rose hands him a mug of steaming coffee.

"We'll hit the hard stuff later." She winks and I groan as I sense the two of them sharing many nights with a whiskey bottle between them and tales of MC clubs and bikers littering the conversation.

Aunt Rose hands me a coffee and sits down opposite. "Carla will come round soon enough; she doesn't know you like we do."

"You think you know me?"

Slade grins and Aunt Rose fixes him with a sharp look. "I probably know you better than you know yourself, if you're anything like Billy. I'm guessing you must be a shade of him for Skye to even look at you."

I feel a warm feeling inside as I think about my future with him. Just sitting here with Slade beside me and my aunt sitting opposite; my mom working in the bar, it feels like home.

"So, what are your plans regarding our visitor later?"

My aunt looks interested and Slade shrugs. "Haven't got one, I figured if he shows up, we'll deal with it outside."

"What do you mean?" I look at him anxiously because if Slade gets into a fight with Devon over me, I can't see it ending well for anyone.

He winks cockily. "It will be fine, the last thing we need is to scare your customers away. Devon's a cool guy, he'll understand."

I'm not so sure of that, but have to trust Slade's judgment on this.

After a while, my aunt heads off to help mom, leaving the

two of us curled up on the couch and this is what I've been waiting for—some time alone.

As soon as the door closes, he turns and grins, "I thought she'd never leave."

As my lips find his, it's all I really want and just the memory of how he can make me feel, is enough to make me whisper, "We could go to my room, they won't disturb us there."

"Darlin', that is the best offer I've ever had, but it will have to wait."

"Why?" I think the hurt must show in my eyes because he says darkly, "I need to be ready for Devon and he could show up at any moment. It wouldn't look good in front of your mom, or your aunt, if I'm zipping up my pants when they call."

"I thought you were bad, now I know you're scared of two women."

He winks. "They scare me, I'm not gonna lie. I see where you get your fire from."

"So, what's going to happen with us, I mean, how will this work?"

I'm anxious to learn just where I fit into his life, and he cups my face in his hands and stares deep into my eyes. "It will always be day one with us, Skye. This feeling, this yearning to make something work so badly, the way we feel around each other, the fact I want to rip your clothes off and fuck you senseless. We will wake up with that feeling every day for the rest of our lives because I never want to lose this feeling inside."

My eyes glitter as I whisper, "It sounds exhausting."

"It will be because I'm insatiable where you're concerned, and you had better have room for me in your bed because the thought of sleeping anywhere else isn't gonna happen."

"But my mom, Aunt Rose."

"Then we will go to the Dragon's Ruin where I intend on showing you all night if necessary, just how much you mean to me."

He kisses me softly, awakening the desire in me like a lit trail of gunpowder. I want him so much, now if it was possible, but I know he's right. We must wait because we have to settle the outstanding problem of a very persistent biker.

I suppose it's only twenty minutes later that my aunt pops her head around the door and says ominously, "He's here."

CHAPTER 33

SLADE

Thank fuck for that, I'm going out of mind with lust for the woman I've been trying to do the right thing by.

Just sitting with her in her family home is something I never do—for anyone. If my brother could see me now, he would die laughing; this isn't me, trying to impress a lady's family because it's vital they like me. I know how close Skye is to her family, and it means a lot. I want to show her I can be that man in her dreams. The one who puts her needs above his and I'm not lying, it's hard. All I want is to throw her on the back of my Harley and take her to the Dragon's Ruin. Be inside her for most of the night and demonstrate how much she means to me the only way I know how.

Now at least Santiago has shown up and we can move this on, so I say roughly, "Stay here, both of you."

I don't look back and head outside and hear him before I see him. "If you could tell her Devon's here, I would appreciate it."

"I've told you." I hear the distaste in her mom's voice and

picture her disapproving look. "Skye is resting because she's had a bad day. I'll tell her you called but…"

I head into the bar and the shock on Devon's face almost makes me laugh out loud as he hisses, "Slade."

"Devon."

I face him off and can feel, rather than see Carla's disapproval.

"What's your business here?"

I pretend I don't know and his eyes narrow.

"Maybe I should say the same thing."

"I'm not here on business, I'm hanging out with my soon to be old lady."

"What, Demi's here?"

Devon looks behind me and I laugh softly. "No, not the one you tried to thrust upon me, the one I was always meant to be with, Skye."

Carla gasps and Devon says angrily, "Since when, she was out with me last night and seemed pretty keen."

"Um, guys," Carla sounds nervous. "Can you take your, um, business, outside please, I do have customers who don't need a floor show."

"It would be my pleasure." Devon turns on his heels and strides angrily from the bar and I laugh softly, "He's not taking this well."

Carla says in a low voice, "Look, I'm not sure what's going on, but my only concern is Skye in all this. Don't make a bad situation worse, and what the hell is all this about an old lady?"

"Don't worry." I smile at the woman who I know only has her daughter's best interests at heart.

"Skye is also my main concern and I won't do anything to hurt her, or your family."

I head outside and see Devon lighting a cigarette, looking extremely angry and he growls, "You had better be playing me Slade because when I left Skye last night, she was more than willing if you know what I mean."

I know he's trying to make me angry, so I don't react and just snarl, "What can I say, we had a fight."

"Do you really expect me to believe that?"

He shakes his head. "I know what this is, you got word Skye was interested in me and came calling. I'm also guessing she's having none of it, judging by her mom's expression, so why don't you get the hell out of here and back to my sister because I haven't forgotten you're meant to be making an honest woman of her."

I shake my head and try to be reasonable.

"About your sister," His eyes narrow.

"Like I said before, I was not the man responsible for how she was that night. You just thought I was, and she didn't correct you. Turns out, she's into way more serious shit than me, so if I were you, I would lock her up and throw away the key if you value her safety."

"Don't you talk to me about family."

Devon is incensed but I know I've struck a nerve because at the mention of Demi's situation he looked worried. "My sister has been her own person since the cradle, nothing can get through to her and I thought…"

He rakes his fingers through his hair and for the first time since meeting him and that's been a number of years, I see the cracks in Devon Santiago. Obviously, family means more to him than he's letting on, and I suppose if I had a sister, I'd be the same.

"You thought what?" My tone is even, but something has shifted between us and he sighs and fixes me with a look that shows his suffering where it concerns her.

"I thought if anyone understood, it was you. Somehow, delivering her to you would guarantee her safety. But it appears I got that wrong because you care more about scoring points against me than you do my sister."

"This isn't about scoring points against you, Devon. It's about my feelings for Skye."

"Feelings." He laughs and a little of the fire returns. "You don't have feelings. You fuck up your women and ruin them for anyone else. Somehow, you crawl inside their soul and cut them wide open. That's what you have in common with my sister and if anything, I thought you would cancel that out in each other."

"So, you sent her to me out of concern for us both. Don't make me laugh, you just wanted her off your hands. Trouble is, that woman is planning on doing just that and you won't like whose hands she falls into."

"What are you talking about?"

"Ask her. What did you once tell me not long ago, on this same spot in fact? I make a good friend but one hell of an enemy. Well, right back at you. Leave Skye and her family alone. I claimed that woman already and what can I say, my feelings for her have surprised me."

He laughs bitterly. "Feelings. You don't know the meaning of the word. You know, Slade, I could almost believe you. Accept I was too late and step away. The thing is, I don't - believe you. You only want Skye because I do, and you want an excuse to ditch the problem I delivered to your club. Well, if Skye Slater is your woman and the object of every fantasy you ever had—prove it."

"How?"

I think the guy must have lost his mind because he's asking for something that's impossible.

"Fetch her and we'll ask her. I want to see the expression in her eye as she tells me to back off. You must forgive me if I don't take your word for it; I need to hear it from the lady herself."

"You doubting my word?"

I stare at him with fury flashing from my eyes and he snarls, "You bet your fucking life I doubt you."

I take a step closer because god help me, I want to smash something, preferably him, but before things go from very bad to a definite bad idea, I hear a soft, "I'll tell you."

CHAPTER 34

SKYE

I had to follow him out. Just the thought of Slade getting hurt in my name was enough to send me running. Aunt Rose tried to stop me but I begged her to let me help and I suppose out of everyone, she understands this world more than most, so she stepped aside. Devon wants proof and I know Slade will struggle with that, so I step forward and say firmly, "I need a word with Devon."

Slade looks as if he's going to tear him apart and Devon is facing him off ready to do battle and I'm so tired of it all.

Moving down the steps, I say quickly, "It's true, Devon, I'm in love with Slade."

The look on Slade's face will stay in my mind forever because he looks so emotional, I feel like crying. I'm guessing love doesn't figure much in his life and hearing someone declare it openly, in front of a man who probably doesn't deal much in love himself, has shaken him.

"I didn't mean for it to happen. It hit me out of nowhere, but it hit me hard. The night I went out with you, Slade was right, I thought we were finished before we even began. He told me to stay away, and I was hurting. He did that because he didn't want me involved in this world you live in. He wanted to keep me safe, and I misinterpreted that for disinterest. I suppose I thought I had run out of options."

He winces a little and I smile. "I'm sorry, that sounded harsh, but I was hurting."

I step before him and say softly, "Just for the record, you did nothing wrong. Any woman would be proud to have you by her side. You were right, you do treat your women well, and I appreciated that. But Slade had already run off with my heart and I was fearful I would never get it back. So, please, Devon, walk away. Don't do this because I'm a lost cause. Against all the odds, I have fallen in love with someone I never dreamed of finding. Someone I can't breathe without thinking of and if you ever find someone like that, you will know how lucky you were that we walked away from this."

Devon nods and I know he understands and his eyes turn to Slade standing beside me, trying so hard to remain impassive, but I can feel the emotion in him as if I know every thought inside his head.

Devon nods but then says darkly, "If that's true, Skye, then I will walk away but there is one thing left that will prove your words."

Slade shifts beside me and I can feel his anger as Devon says darkly, "If you have been with Slade, there will be evidence on your body. Show me that he claimed you because until I see that mark, I will not believe a word of what you just said and know that I've been lied to."

"NO!" Slade steps between us and growls, "You doubting her word?"

"Yes."

Devon faces him and I say quickly, "Ok."

Slade looks around in shock and I know what he's thinking and I smile, the tears burning brightly in my eyes.

"You wouldn't mark me, Slade."

Devon laughs softly, "I knew it."

Ignoring him, I stare deep into Slade's eyes and say nervously, "I begged you to. I wanted the whole of you. I wanted what you had given every girl before me and I wanted more. You held back something you thought worth nothing. You couldn't bring yourself to mark my skin; to cut me and cause me pain. I didn't understand at the time, I thought you didn't care, thought me unworthy to bear your mark, but I wanted it so badly - needed it so badly, to see you every time I looked in the mirror. A physical reminder of how good things are between us, the mark of being your woman, but you couldn't do it. Perhaps that told me this was special. I had made you feel something nobody else ever had, or that you didn't want me. When you pushed me away, I thought it was that. I wasn't worthy; I meant nothing to you. Well, I went there anyway because despite what you wanted, I needed to remember you had taught me something I would never forget."

Taking his hands, I stare into his eyes and it's as if Devon is no longer here. "I wanted a permanent reminder of the man I fell in love with. Who taught me what love is and how beautiful it is when you find it."

Stepping back, I lift my skirt and look into his eyes as he sees just what I did in the name of love for him. He just stares in shock as I reveal the reason I went to see my brother before visiting my parents.

He steps forward and traces the ink on my skin in wonder as if he can't believe what he's seeing and I look down at his hand on the tattoo of the dragon with our initials entwined, a scar breaking through the middle of it showing that love can be tarnished but beautiful because of it.

He drops to his knees and presses his lips to the image

and the tears spill down my cheeks as he worships what I did for him—for me—for us.

I look up and see Devon watching the scene and I know he understands because our eyes meet and he nods before turning and walking away. Leaving us standing in the open air, two opposites that fate decided were worthy of a shot at love.

Slade holds me close and I feel his breath on my skin, on the image I had created especially for us. Grady did everything in his power to talk me out of this. Threatened me with my parents; told me he wouldn't do it. It was only when I told him I'd get it done elsewhere, he gave in and even if I had never seen Slade again, I wanted to see the moment I fell in love with a man who changed me inside forever. Made me a woman and made me realize how amazing love is.

He stands and holds my face in his two hands gently and whispers, "You did that for me?"

I nod. "And me. I couldn't walk away because you didn't just teach me sex, Slade, you taught me love. I know you never intended on that, but it happened, anyway. You taught me that one shouldn't go without the other. It's so magical and they need each other to work properly. Sex without love is painful, disturbing, and leaves an open wound. When you fall in love, it's the most beautiful feeling in the world and drives addiction. You devastated me, Slade. You took my emotions and trampled on them. You tore me open and walked away while I bled at your feet. When I heard you had an old lady, I was destroyed. The reason I went with Devon was to plug the void you left. To try to fill it with a lesser version of you. I told myself it was revenge, it wasn't. It was because if I couldn't have you, I wanted something *like* you."

I laugh softly, "That was my big mistake because there is nothing like you, Slade Channing, not even close."

Leaning forward, I press my lips to his, desperate to feel

them against me. As his hand wraps around my head and kisses me hard, deeply and with passion, my heart breathes easy. It's true, not every girl loves a bad boy because I know in my heart Slade isn't bad. He's just lost something I hope I can help him find, and I will spend my whole life trying.

CHAPTER 35

SLADE

Skye has blown me away completely. That tattoo, the way she faced Devon and declared her love for me, will be something I never forget. I could kiss her all night, but then I hear a loud, "Put her down and come inside. We have some celebrating to do."

We break apart and I look up in surprise and see Rose and Clara watching us from the door. The smiles on their faces tell me they heard every word and Skye grins, "God, how embarrassing is this?"

She buries her face in my chest and I wrap my arms around her and whisper, "Come on, let's drink Rose under the table because I'm impatient to be alone with you."

She shivers against me. "Me too."

Taking her hand, we walk toward her family who have smiles instead of worry on their faces and Skye looks at her mom nervously. "Mom... I..."

Clara just smiles through her tears and holds out her arms. "It's ok, baby girl. Your happiness is everything to me and if Slade makes you happy, then so am I."

Seeing Skye with her mom makes me think of my

own, and it's a hard feeling to deal with. Rose steps closer and holds out her arms and to my surprise, pulls me into them and whispers, "A mother's love is a beautiful thing that never dies. She lives inside you, Slade, always remember that, she is a part of you as much as your father. You will carry her with you all your life and never forget that."

I'm not sure how I ended up here, but it feels good. For so long I've been alone, dealing with emotions I couldn't understand. Anger, pain, desperation and hatred that have been swept away by one important one. Love.

Love from strangers—for strangers who owe me nothing. Love of a woman I nearly lost because of a stupid sense of doing something right for once, ignoring the fact the right thing to do was keep her by my side.

Now we can start again, and I'm impatient for that. Wanting to keep her with me, close to me, love her every minute I can and so, as we head inside, I plan on doing that just as soon as possible.

It's a strange evening because after drinking whiskey with Rose while Skye helped her mother in the bar, we end up sitting in the same booth that I found her in the night I first came. Her mom and aunt have gone to bed, leaving us wrapped in shadows and drinking coffee, making plans and making out.

But that's not enough because I need to show, rather than tell, so I whisper, "Show me your bedroom."

Her breathing intensifies and she whispers, "What about mom, she's a light sleeper?"

"Then this will have to do."

"What here?"

I nod. "Let's start where we began."

"That doesn't make sense." She laughs softly, and it makes me smile.

"It makes perfect sense. I found you here in this booth, not that long ago as it happens."

"A lot has happened since then."

"Important things have happened."

She presses her lips to mine and whispers huskily, "Amazing things."

She shifts onto my lap and wraps her arms around me, pressing into me, making me lose my mind a little."

"So, what happens now?"

"Well, first…" I lift her top and remove it and love how heavy with desire her eyes are.

"I kiss you here." Running my tongue against her skin, I love the way she shivers as I lick a trail to the deep valley between her breasts. Reaching behind her, I undo her bra and capture her breasts in my mouth and roll my tongue around her erect nipple. She groans and runs her fingers through my hair. "That feels so good."

She returns the favor and lifts my own t-shirt over my head and rubs her breasts against my chest, almost purring with pleasure. "You feel so good."

Reaching for her skirt, I unzip the back and she wriggles out of it as she unfastens my jeans and I shift so she can edge them down, along with my underwear and as my cock springs free, she fists it hard and groans. "I've missed you."

"What, me or my cock?"

"Both, but mainly your cock." She giggles and I laugh softly, loving the sound. She grinds against it and says huskily, "What happens next?"

"Well, that depends on what you want the most. Do you want to take it slow, or cut to the chase?"

"Slow."

She grins wickedly and shifts lower and as I feel her lips close around my shaft, it's my turn to groan as I edge inside her hot, sweet mouth and feel her sucking, licking and squeezing my throbbing cock. As I thrust inside, she moans against it and it feels good seeing her silky hair draped around my cock, feeling her owning and claiming me as hers and I never knew it could be this emotional.

Just feeling her tongue and the way she sucks noisily, turns me on so much I almost shoot my load down her throat and so I pull her up and say huskily, "Not so fast."

Pushing her down onto the seat, I spread her knees and repay the favor, and as my own tongue finds her honey, it's my turn to groan in pleasure when she gasps as I find her sweetest spot. Just before she comes, I pull her up and reach for a condom in my jeans and quickly sheaf my cock before saying, "Sit on me."

She nods and hitches her breath, and I know this is the only way to drive a bad memory away. Lifting her hips, I lower her carefully onto my cock and feel myself sliding inside her honey coated walls. She bites her bottom lip and groans, not with pain but with pure pleasure, as she fits around my cock perfectly. I am so deep inside Skye, I feel her soul and as she gently rides it, I stare at a sight that is so beautiful I want to see the whole of it. The moonlight shines through the window and lights up a face I want to see every day of my life. Beautiful, sensuous and perfect, a goddess that fate thought I deserved. Just watching Skye experience the pleasure I can give her makes me harder and as she cries out, I fasten my lips to hers to absorb the sound.

This is gentle love, not rough sex. A meeting of hearts wrapped up in physical pleasure. So much pleasure and as she comes apart all over my cock, I shoot up inside her so hard I lose my mind for a moment. Soon I will know what it feels like to mark my woman inside, not outside because the first thing is to get us checked out and Skye on birth control because until my seed coats her inside, I won't be happy.

I don't need to cut her skin; I need to fill her with my seed and one day make it count. Grow something that will be the result of love and I will never walk away from that. Any child of mine will know what it feels like to have two parents who love unconditionally, and their only addiction is for each other. That's the vow I make to this woman because she deserves it, and so do I.

CHAPTER 36

SKYE

The Dragon's Ruin. The last time I was here, I never went inside. That day I rode off with a cold unfeeling monster who taught me how to love. A special time that we have plans to recreate, but not today. Today I'm going to work with my man and he is going to introduce me to his world, *my world* because I am determined to share the whole of him and if that means understanding and living in an MC club, then that's fine by me.

Slade helps me off the bike and removes my helmet and I love seeing the wild look in his eyes as he crushes his lips to mine. "Welcome home, darlin'." He growls against my lips and I'm already wet for him. I'm always wet for him which gets a little uncomfortable at times, but I'll live with that.

He takes my hand and I see a couple of bikers watching us from the yard and Slade says loudly, "Hey, Gibbs, Joe, this is Skye, soon to be my old lady, so keep your fucking eyes off her."

They laugh and head our way and I shiver inside. This is it; they look so scary I grip Slade's hand a little tighter and say shyly, "I'm pleased to meet you."

"Same darlin'." One of them smiles and the other nods. "Welcome to the Dragon's Ruin, please accept my apology."

"What for?"

"For anything you may see or hear inside. We're trying, but old habits die hard."

He laughs and Slade growls, "We're not fucking saints, some things will ever change."

He sighs and says to the quieter one, "Is Marina here?"

A slow smile breaks out across the guy's face, "Yes, sorry man, I guess she's about to have a very bad day."

He looks at me sympathetically. "She'll learn, honey, give her some time."

Slade shrugs. "That's her problem, not mine."

Turning to me, he grins. "Well, what are we waiting for, it's time to bring you home?"

He sweeps me into his arms and the guys laugh as he carries me up the steps and laughs. "You can't escape now."

"Who said I wanted to?"

I kiss him with a hunger that never goes away and as we fall inside laughing, I hear, "About fucking time you showed up."

Slade lowers me to the ground and I look at an attractive woman with the most beautiful red hair, looking at me with interest. Slade laughs softly beside me as she steps forward and, to my surprise, pulls me in for a hug. "Welcome honey, thank God you came."

She pulls back and laughs at the astonishment on my face. "Hi, I'm Marina. General dogsbody and well, we won't go into that right now, but I never thought I'd meet a woman who tamed the beast."

She winks and looks at Slade with a longing I don't miss. "It had to happen, I suppose, and if it's worth anything, I'm happy for you–both of you."

She seems a little upset and I look at Slade in confusion and to my surprise he says to her sweetly, "You ok, honey?"

"I'm good, more than good, relieved actually, because now I know there's absolutely no possible chance for me, I'm free to find someone better."

She winks and then says brightly, "I'm sorry, Skye, isn't it? You should know I've had designs on Slade since I came here. The trouble is, he didn't want me, so it's something I've had to live with. Don't feel bad about that, its common knowledge and one of the bitches inside probably can't wait to tell you, but I'm telling you now, I'll be a good friend to you here. Now, come on in and I'll make you some coffee, throw a shot of whiskey your way, you name it, I'll provide it."

She takes my arm and whisks me inside, leaving Slade to follow, looking a little bemused.

As we walk, she explains where we are and I stare in surprise at a place that looks nothing like I imagined. It's clean, tidy and I can tell she's tried to make it homey, and is a far cry from the tales I've heard of a dirty biker paradise with whores dripping from the walls and bleeding on the floors.

Even the bar looks pleasant and clean, and she looks around with obvious pride.

"You're lucky you're here now and not three months ago. You'd have run screaming from this place. It's different now Slade's president, the guys fear and respect him, so shaped up a little and it's now considered an honor to be a dragon."

"Have you been here long?"

"A while. When I first came here, I paired up with Slade." She must see my face fall because she says sadly, "For one night only. Then I grabbed the attention of his uncle Axel, who's on a road trip. You know, it's not been easy at times but despite it all, I love it here, which is why I want us to get along."

"Why would that affect you?"

She smiles sadly. "Because you'll be the president's old lady and what you say goes. I don't want us to be at odds with each other, and I want to be the best friend you have here. Slade, well..."

We look across and see him talking to one of the guys, and Marina's eyes soften. "He hides it well, but he's wearing a battered soul. I think he needs someone like you to make him the man we all know he can be. I'm not sure if you intend on living here with him, but I'm guessing you will because unlike his father, Slade won't want to hide you away, so I guess we'll be seeing a lot of you around here."

I look around and it's not so bad. When Rose spoke of the place, she described it as hell on earth. It's ok, perhaps could use a little money spent on it but nothing as she described and I suppose that's down to the woman who is trying her best to make me feel welcome.

So, I smile brightly and say warmly, "I won't interfere in a thing because I have my own bar to run. I'd like to be of help though when I am here, so you just point me in the right direction and I'll do my best."

Marina looks relieved and grins. "First stop coffee and then I'm guessing your man will want some of your time, what can I say, you're one lucky girl."

If it feels strange having another woman obviously lusting after my man, I push it away because Marina talks with an acceptance of how things are. In a way, I'm glad of it because she's open and honest and I suppose she wants that to be the basis of our friendship and looking around, it's obvious I need as many friends here as I can get.

CHAPTER 37

SLADE

Seeing Skye in the Castle is the weirdest feeling. Part of me hates that she's here because she's too good for this place. Then again, I hate the thought of her anywhere else because I want to keep my eyes on her 24/7 because if anything ever happened to her because of me, I would never forgive myself.

I leave her to talk to Marina to form a strong bond because Marina is an important member of the team. The fact she has taken Skye under her wing means everything to me, and just the sound of Skye's laughter as she listens to Marina speak, touches me deep inside.

For the first time, I see a future for the Dragon's Ruin. A home and a place for the Dragons to live and be happy. We couldn't go on like we were. Something had to give and Skye has entered this place like a beautiful rainbow, with a very promising pot of gold at the end.

With her beside me, I can achieve anything and our life starts here. I have my club; I have my family but most of all I have her and now I can't wait to show her what that means.

I give her one hour, but that's all because I need her by my side more than anything, so I go and find her and whisper, "You're coming with me."

Her hand curls around mine and it's like a physical blow to my heart. Just knowing what my life will be like with her beside me, has changed me so much I don't recognize myself anymore.

As we walk to the office, I say casually, "Do you think Grady would mind repeating your tattoo on me?"

She stops and stares at me in surprise. "Really?"

I nod and she smiles so brightly I need my shades against the glare. "You would do that, for me?"

"I would do anything for you."

I pull her tight and grip her hard, loving how she feels so good against me. Dipping my head, I nip her neck and groan. "The only thing you get to decide is where?"

"Anywhere?" She grins as I nod.

"Anywhere."

"So, if I decided I wanted it on your face, how would you feel about that?"

"I would think it a little strange but you get to decide, I'm a man of my word."

She giggles and strokes my cheek lightly, which is enough to have me deciding whether to push her against the wall and fuck her in the hall.

She traces her fingers down my face to my neck and whispers, "What about here?"

She presses her lips to my neck and I shiver inside.

"If you like."

She flashes me a wicked look and lifts up my top and presses her lips to my chest. "How about here?"

"Better." I struggle to breathe as she drops to her knees and unfastens my pants and whispers, "What about here, it could be painful."

She frees my cock and I look up the hall and listen for footsteps because god help them if they come around the corner right now.

Her mouth closes around my cock and I hiss, loving the feeling of her teeth grazing my throbbing shaft.

She draws me in and sucks, and I stop breathing.

Grabbing my ass, she pulls me in and guides me deeper, sucking, licking, tasting.

"Skye, honey, I…"

She clamps her mouth tighter and pulls me in so deep, I feel the back of her throat and I can't help but shoot my load so fast, I roar like an animal.

To her credit, she takes it all, every last fucking drop, and I run my fingers through her hair, loving seeing it draped around my cock.

As soon as I'm spent, she licks it clean and pulls my pants up, before grinning wickedly, "I haven't decided where yet, I may need some time to discover where I think it will look best."

For a moment we just stare at each other, stupid grins on our faces as we face an exciting future. Skye and Slade intertwined in ink and hearts and I never realized what an amazing woman fate had planned for me.

She slips her hand in mine and flutters those gorgeous eyelashes before saying huskily, "Now show me your office, I have an urge to make some memories of our own in there."

Lifting her hand to my mouth, I kiss it gently and whisper, "I love you Skye Slater, so hard it hurts but I will love Skye Channing until the day I die."

She blinks and then laughs. "You're presuming rather a lot there, biker, I wasn't aware I agreed to that."

"You're my woman, Skye, get used to it."

I grin to take the arrogance from my words and she nods.

"I wouldn't want it any other way, so, why don't you show me what all the fuss is about?"

As we head toward my office, I'm intending on doing just that for the rest of my life.

The End

ALSO BY STELLA ANDREWS

If you didn't read Slade after Catch a King, you may want to see what happened before he met Skye.

Catch up with his family & start a series that will take your breath away.

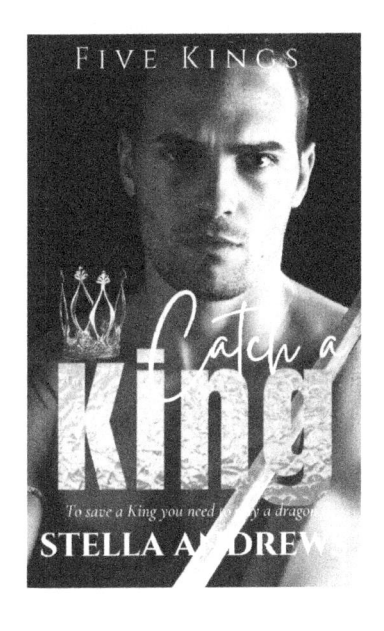

Read Now

~

Coming Soon – Pre-order now

Steal a King

FIVE KINGS

To steal a King you need to catch a thief

STELLA ANDREWS

STAY IN TOUCH

Reasons to sign up to my mailing list.

A reminder that you can read my books FREE with Kindle Unlimited.

Receive a monthly newsletter so you don't miss out on any special offers or new releases.

Links to follow me on Amazon or social media to be kept up to date with new releases.

Grab your free copy of The Highest Bidder as a thank you for signing up to my newsletter.

Opportunities to read my books before they are even released by joining my team.

Sneak peeks at new material before anyone else.

stellaandrews.com
Follow me on Amazon

BOOKS BY STELLA ANDREWS

Twisted Reapers
Daddy's Girls (Ryder & Ashton)
Twisted (Sam & Kitty)
The Billion Dollar baby (Tyler & Sydney)
Bodyguard (Jet & Lucy)
Flash (Flash & Jennifer)
Country Girl (Tyson & Sunny)
Standalone
The Highest Bidder (Logan & Samantha)
Rocked (Jax & Emily)
Bad Influence (Max & Summer)
Deck the Boss
Beauty Series
Breaking Beauty (Sebastian & Angel) *
Owning Beauty (Tobias & Anastasia)
Broken Beauty (Maverick & Sophia) *
The Romanos
The Throne of Pain (Lucian & Riley)
The Throne of Hate (Dante & Isabella)
The Throne of Fear (Romeo & Ivy)
Lorenzo's story is in Broken Beauty
Five Kings
<u>Catch a King (Sawyer & Millie) *</u>
<u>Slade</u>
<u>* = Connected to Twisted Reapers</u>

Coming Soon

Steal a King

BEFORE YOU GO

Thank you for reading this story.
If you have enjoyed the fantasy world of this novel please would you be so kind as to leave a review on Amazon?

Join my closed Facebook Group

Stella's Sexy Readers

Follow me on Instagram

Stay healthy and happy and thanks for reading xx

Made in the USA
Middletown, DE
20 March 2024

Diet and Nutrition for Bodybuilding

The Ultimate Bodybuilding Diet and Nutrition Manual

Bodybuilding Diet & Nutrition tips, plans, foods, and more for building your best body!

By: Jon Shelton

Copyrights and Trademarks

All rights reserved. No part of this book may be reproduced or transformed in any form or by any means, graphic, electronic, or mechanical, including photocopying, recording, taping, or by any information storage retrieval system, without the written permission of the author.

This publication is Copyright ©2015 NRB Publishing, an imprint of Pack & Post Plus, LLC. Nevada. All products, graphics, publications, software and services mentioned and recommended in this publication are protected by trademarks. In such instance, all trademarks & copyright belong to the respective owners. For information consult www.NRBpublishing.com

Disclaimer and Legal Notice

This product is not legal, medical, or accounting advice and should not be interpreted in that manner. You need to do your own due-diligence to determine if the content of this product is right for you. While every attempt has been made to verify the information shared in this publication, neither the author, neither publisher, nor the affiliates assume any responsibility for errors, omissions or contrary interpretation of the subject matter herein. Any perceived slights to any specific person(s) or organization(s) are purely unintentional.

We have no control over the nature, content and availability of the web sites listed in this book. The inclusion of any web site links does not necessarily imply a recommendation or endorse the views expressed within them. We take no responsibility for, and will not be liable for, the websites being temporarily unavailable or being removed from the internet.

The accuracy and completeness of information provided herein and opinions stated herein are not guaranteed or warranted to produce any particular results, and the advice and strategies, contained herein may not be suitable for every individual. Neither the author nor the publisher shall be liable for any loss incurred as a consequence of the use and application, directly or indirectly, of any information presented in this work. This publication is designed to provide information in regard to the subject matter covered.

Neither the author nor the publisher assume any responsibility for any errors or omissions, nor do they represent or warrant that the ideas, information, actions, plans, suggestions contained in this book is in all cases accurate. It is the reader's responsibility to find advice before putting anything written in this book into practice. The information in this book is not intended to serve as legal, medical, or accounting advice.